W9-CNA-835

Computer Crime

Issues in Focus

Computer Crime

Phreaks, Spies, and Salami Slicers

Revised Edition

30036000596997

Karen Judson

Enslow Publishers, Inc.

40 Industrial Road	PO Box 38
Box 398	Aldershot
Berkeley Heights, NJ 07922	Hants GU12 6BP
USA	UK

http://www.enslow.com

Library of Congress Cataloging–in–Publication Data

Judson, Karen, 1941–
    Computer crime : phreaks, spies, and salami slicers / Karen
Judson. — Rev. ed.
        p. cm. — (Issues in focus)
    Includes bibliographical references and index.
    Summary: Describes different computer crimes, including hacking,
computer fraud, viruses, and Internet scams, discussing the methods
used to commit them and penalties for those who are caught.
    ISBN 0-7660-1243-3
    1. Computer crimes Juvenile literature. [1. Computer crimes.]
I. Title. II. Series: Issues in focus (Hillside, N.J.)
HV6773.J83   2000
364.16'8—dc21   99-15596
                                                     CIP

Printed in the United States of America

10 9 8 7 6 5 4 3 2

To Our Readers:
All Internet addresses in this book were active and appropriate when
we went to press. Any comments or suggestions can be sent by e-mail
to comments@enslow.com or to the address on the back cover.

Illustration Credits:
Chris Sciacca, p. 108; © Corel Corporation, pp. 83, 97;
Courtesy of the FBI, p. 77; Courtesy of Intel Corporation, p. 31;
Enslow Publishers, Inc., p. 87; IBM Archives, Somers, N.Y., pp.
26, 29; Karen Judson, p. 61; Mark Beal, Texas Engineering
Experiment Station, p. 45; Mitsubishi Electric, from the Library
of Congress Photoduplication Service, p. 21; Robert E.
Kalmbach, University of Michigan, p. 51; U.S. Army, p. 23.

Cover Illustration: ©The Stock Market / Michael Newler, 1991

Contents

1

Arrested!

On February 15, 1995, thirty-one-year-old Kevin Mitnick shuffled into a courtroom in Raleigh, North Carolina. People who saw his shackled wrists and feet may have thought that he was a dangerous murderer. Mitnick was no murderer, but he was in serious trouble. He had been captured the night before by federal agents. They had chased him for two years for alleged crimes ranging from parole violations to illegally tampering with telephones and computers.

The Raleigh judge read the charges against Mitnick: twenty-three counts of telecommunications fraud and computer fraud. Each charge carried a maximum possible sentence of fifteen years or more in prison.

Mitnick's trouble with the law dated back to the 1970s and early 1980s when he was a teenager living in Los Angeles, California. He was fascinated by computers, and by age thirteen he had learned how to electronically break into telephone company computers. Once in, he could download technical files, set up free accounts, impersonate directory assistance, or otherwise tamper with telephone service. He eventually expanded his break-ins to other large computer systems. By 1995, Mitnick had been arrested and convicted five times for:

- stealing operators' manuals from Pacific Bell Telephone and destroying data over a computer network;

- digitally altering connections to receive free long-distance telephone services;

- illegally entering Pentagon computers;

- electronically stealing software from a California software company;

- committing computer fraud and possessing illegal long-distance access codes.[1]

Mitnick was also credited with several alleged acts of revenge, such as altering the credit information of a judge, disconnecting the telephone of a probation officer, and planting a false story on a financial news network about a company that had refused him a job.[2]

At first, because of his youth, Mitnick was placed

on probation for his crimes. Then at seventeen he served three months in a juvenile detention center, followed by a year's probation. In 1983, after a conviction for breaking into a Pentagon computer, he served six months in a juvenile prison called the California Youth Authority's Karl Holton Training School in Stockton, California. Finally, a 1989 conviction for computer fraud resulted in a one-year term in a federal prison in California. After Mitnick was released, he spent six months in a court-ordered program for his computer "addiction."[3]

After that, Mitnick worked as a computer programmer, but he could not resist breaking into computer systems. Another warrant was issued for his arrest in 1992 for violating the terms of his 1989 probation. He fled California and dropped out of sight.

Mitnick was soon up to his old tricks, however. His downfall began on Christmas Day, 1994, when he penetrated the computers of Tsutomu Shimomura, a computational physicist and computer security expert at the San Diego Supercomputer Center, a federally financed research facility.

Not only was the thirty-year-old Shimomura a brilliant physicist, he had earned a reputation as a security software designer and consultant to corporations, the FBI, the U.S. Air Force, the National Security Agency, and others. When he learned that his computers had been violated on Christmas Day, 1994, he and his colleagues began a determined search for the intruders. On December 26, Andrew Gross, a graduate student at the University of

California at San Diego who worked with Shimomura, found that computer logs had been edited to hide a break-in. Gross notified Shimomura, who was headed for a ski vacation in the Sierra Nevada mountains.

His vacation cut short, Shimomura and his coworkers pored over computer logs for traces left behind by the attackers. Then on January 27, 1995, Bruce Koball, a Berkeley, California, software designer, discovered hundreds of megabytes of software stashed in an account he sometimes used on the Well, a Sausalito, California, online service. He had recently read an article about the Shimomura incident in *The New York Times*, and he recognized the data in his Well account as Shimomura's stolen software and e-mail. He notified Shimomura, who then requested that the Well remove the stolen data.

By February 7, 1995, it was clear that the intruder was using the Well as a staging base for attacks on various university and corporate computers. On February 9, 1995, the trail from the Well led to Netcom Online Communications Services, an Internet service provider located in San Jose, California. Shimomura went to San Jose and set up a monitoring system he had designed. He and other investigators watched as the intruder deprogrammed telephone circuits, electronically copied files from Motorola, Apple Computer, and other companies, and stole over twenty thousand credit card numbers from one online data base.[4]

Certain clues had led investigators to suspect Mitnick as the intruder. Then on February 10,

Shimomura identified Kevin Mitnick as the intruder when Mitnick complained via e-mail to a correspondent in Israel that his picture had appeared in *The New York Times*.

While monitoring at Netcom, Shimomura noted that the intruder most often appeared from Raleigh, North Carolina. On February 11, he enlisted the help of Sprint cellular telephone engineers in Raleigh. They found that, to mask his location, Mitnick had tampered with the local GTE telephone switching system. Shimomura and Sprint engineers compared database records from Netcom with calls made from the cellular system to find the Raleigh location of the person making the cellular calls.

On February 12, 1995, Shimomura flew to Raleigh, where he met with Sprint cellular engineers. That night, he and the engineers drove through the Raleigh suburbs, using cellular telephone diagnostic equipment to pick up calls made by Mitnick. They pinned down his location to an apartment complex about one mile from the Raleigh airport.

On February 14, FBI agents staked out the Raleigh apartment complex. Using a handheld signal strength meter, they found the apartment where calls to Netcom were originating.[5]

On February 15, seven weeks after Shimomura joined the search for Mitnick, he was present when agents closed in on the man whom a Justice Department spokesperson had called an "information terrorist."[6] Not only had Shimomura been the victim of computer theft, but from December 27, 1994 through February 15, 1995 he had also received six anonymous voice mail messages. Speaking with an exaggerated Asian accent, the caller had taunted, "Your technique is no good," and had threatened "We'll kill you." In two messages received on February 15, the caller had protested that "this is getting too big," and had pleaded with Shimomura not to contact the FBI.[7]

Shortly after Mitnick's arrest Shimomura told newspaper reporters, "I'm curious to know what's broken in him, why he feels compelled to do this."[8]

After his 1995 arrest in North Carolina, Mitnick pleaded guilty to one charge of cellular telephone fraud. He was sentenced to eight months in prison. He was then transferred from North Carolina to Los Angeles, California. There he faced additional charges, including federal probation violations, tampering with computers of the California Department of Motor Vehicles, and other computer and telephone fraud charges.

In prison in California, Mitnick was denied bail and was refused use of a computer or unsupervised use of a telephone. On March 26, 1999, Mitnick pleaded guilty to computer and wire fraud charges, which resolved both federal and state cases against him. The sealed plea agreement reportedly required Mitnick to stay away from computers for four years after his release from jail and barred him from profiting from his story. Mitnick was sentenced in August 1999 to a prison term of forty-six months. He was also fined $4,125. With credit for time served, Mitnick could be released by January 2000.[9]

What Is Computer Crime?

Kevin Mitnick was prosecuted for computer crimes. Although the term *computer crime* does not have a precise definition, it can be classified in three ways:

- A computer is the target of the offense. Unauthorized entry is gained in order to steal information from or cause damage to a computer system or the data it contains.

- A computer is the tool used to commit the offense. In these cases, credit card numbers may be stolen from the data banks of companies; money may be electronically skimmed from bank accounts; or unauthorized electronic transfers of funds may be made from financial institutions.

- Computers are used in a crime but are not actually part of the act. For example, drug dealers or other professional criminals may use computers to store records of illegal transactions.

Computer Crime Laws

Computer criminals break federal laws and sometimes state laws as well. In the United States, there are two main federal laws against computer crime: The Computer Fraud and Abuse Act of 1986 and the Electronic Communications Privacy Act of 1986. A computer crime breaks the Computer Fraud and Abuse Act when it involves:

- stealing or compromising data about national

defense, foreign relations, atomic energy, or other restricted information;

- gaining access to computers owned by any agency or department of the United States government;

- violating data belonging to banks or other financial institutions;

- intercepting or otherwise intruding upon communications between states or foreign countries; or

- threatening to damage computer systems in order to extort money or other valuables from persons, businesses, or institutions.

The act was expanded in 1996 by the Computer Abuse Amendments Act to cover computer viruses and other harmful code.

The Electronic Communications Privacy Act of 1986 prohibits breaking into any electronic communications service, including telephone services. It forbids the interception of any type of electronic communications. *Interception* includes listening in on communications and recording or otherwise taking the contents of communications.

In addition to the two main laws mentioned above, several other federal laws may apply to computer crime. Patent laws protect some software and computer hardware, and contract laws may protect trade secrets that are kept on computers. In 1980 the U.S. Copyright Act was amended to include computer software. It is a violation of this act to post online written compositions, pictures, sound files, and software without the permission of the copyright holder.

The Federal Bureau of Investigation (FBI) and the U.S. Secret Service (USSS) jointly enforce federal computer crime laws. The FBI is in charge when crimes involve espionage, terrorism, banking, organized crime, and threats to national security. The Secret Service investigates crimes against Treasury Department computers and against computers that contain information protected by the Financial Privacy Act. This includes credit card information, credit reporting information, and data kept on bank loan applications. In some federal cases, the Customs Department, Commerce Department, or the military may have jurisdiction.

In addition to federal laws, as of January 1999, forty-nine states had passed laws against computer crime. Vermont was considering but had not yet passed computer crime legislation. Several foreign countries have also passed laws prohibiting computer crime.

Some violations of state and federal computer crime laws may be charged as misdemeanors, punishable by fines of not more than one year in prison. Others are felonies, which are punishable by more than one year in prison.

The Computer Access Issue

The prosecution of Kevin Mitnick and others accused of computer crimes has spotlighted the debate between the two sides of the computer access issue.

On one side are those who favor unrestricted access to information: civil libertarians, the information industry, communications-service providers, and the expert computer users called *hackers*. Prosecute computer criminals, this side says, but don't stifle the free exchange of information.

On the other side of the argument are privacy advocates, government agencies, law enforcement officials, and businesses that depend on the data stored in computers. From their point of view, anyone who breaks into a computer is an electronic Peeping Tom and a trespasser.

In recent years the debate has expanded. The global reach of computer networks has raised questions about copyrights, privacy, and security. How can the ownership rights of those who create software and other copyrighted materials be protected? Do those who gather and store information about individuals, such as financial or health records, own the material, or should it be freely available to those it concerns?

Furthermore, what role should the government play in regulating cyberspace? (The term *cyberspace* refers to computer networks and was first used by science-fiction writer William Gibson in his 1986 novel *Neuromancer*.) Can the government protect computer networks against abuse without destroying those networks? Or without violating civil rights, such as the right to privacy?

How broad should the definition of computer crime be? Should penalties be the same for those who illegally access computers but do no damage as well as for those who destroy, alter, or steal data or services? And what is the definition of "damage"? For example, a digital break-in usually does no physical damage to computers. It does, however, cause the system to close down while software is reloaded and passwords are changed. Should the resulting downtime be counted as damage? Is data truly stolen if it remains on the violated computer after the theft?

Most important, since the smooth functioning of society now depends on computers, can we guarantee the security of electronically stored information yet still preserve personal rights and freedoms?

2

Computerizing Society

Near the end of the second millennium (one thousand years) of the present Western calendar, newspaper headlines warned: "Y2K Bug's Bite Could Be Fatal!" ("Y2K" is an abbreviation for the Year 2000. *Bug* is a slang term referring to a computer error.)

The bug behind the doomsday prophesies resulted from a computer programming shorthand common in the 1960s and 1970s. When many of the current systems running everything from traffic lights to nuclear waste facilities were first programmed, computer memory was limited. To save space, programmers entered years

18

as two digits instead of four. The year 1969 was 69, 1970 was 70, and so on. No one considered what would happen when the year 2000 came, because it was a long way off. It was assumed that the original code written by programmers would be replaced long before then.[1]

Most of the early software was not replaced, however. As the turn of the century neared, experts warned that computers' inability to tell the year 1900 (represented in computer code as 00) from 2000 would cause problems. Some predicted that confused computers would crash. If this were to happen, telephone service, electricity, water purification, and many other vital services would be lost. Government computers handling Social Security, Medicare, income tax, and countless other records would stop. Banking and credit services would be disrupted, maybe causing the collapse of national economic systems.

The predictions of other experts were less gloomy. Some failures would occur, they said, causing short-term disruption of services, but they foresaw no global catastrophe.

Nevertheless, by 1998, computer programmers who could find and replace faulty code were in great demand as everyone raced to beat the January 1, 2000, deadline.

Why the panic when the Y2K bug was brought to public attention? Because computers run almost everything in today's world. In fact, it's hard to remember what life was like before society became so dependent on the machines.

A basic knowledge of how computers were developed and how they work is helpful in understanding society's growing dependence on the machines and why computers have become useful tools for criminals.

Developing the Electronic Brain

The invention of electricity paved the way for modern-day computers because the electric switches inside computers are the key to their performance. Located first in vacuum tubes, then in transistors, the switches open and close when exposed to an electrical current. All electronic computers are run by programs (lists of instructions) that are made up of a complex series of 1s and 0s, called a binary code. The bits (BInary digiTS), or characters in the binary code, command a switch to open or close. When a low-voltage current is applied to a switch, it is read as a zero, and the switch is said to be closed. A high-voltage current represents a one, which opens the switch.

Before the invention of transistors, glass vacuum tubes regulated the flow of electricity inside computers. These tubes were controlled by dozens of switches that had to be set by hand. Once entered in the computer, problems could take days or weeks to solve.

The largest and most powerful electronic vacuum tube computer of its day was the Electronic Numerical Integrator and Computer (ENIAC), built at the University of Pennsylvania in 1946. ENIAC was

Herman Hollerith's electrical tabulator was used to count the U.S. Census in 1890. This photograph, taken in 1908, shows an operator at the keyboard.

designed to provide firing tables for new artillery in World War II. The mammoth machine weighed 27 metric tons and filled a 30- by 50-foot (9- by 15-meter) room. It cost $3,223,846 to build and took 140 kilowatts of power and 18,000 vacuum tubes to run. ENIAC was more than a thousand times faster than any previous computer, but it was so complicated to program and run that its use was severely restricted.[2]

Then in 1958 transistorized computers were introduced, beginning a new era in data processing. Transistors are tiny electronic devices that act as switches by allowing passage of an electrical current or blocking its flow. Transistorized computers were five times faster than the older vacuum-tube models, used less power, and gave off less heat.[3]

Microprocessors Lead to a Second Generation of Computers

When the integrated circuit (IC)—also called a microchip (chip) or microprocessor—was introduced in the late 1960s, computers were again reborn. Integrated circuits allowed many transistors to be placed on one silicon substrate. (Silicon is an abundant element found in rocks and sand.) Intel produced the first microchip, the 4004, in 1971. It contained 2,250 transistors, connected by superfine aluminum wires, embedded in a tiny fleck of silicon. Computers made with the new microchips were small enough to sit on a desktop, and were faster, cheaper, and more reliable than earlier machines.

Two women wiring the right side of the ENIAC with a new program, in the early days of computers.

Throughout the 1970s and 1980s, Intel's 4004 microchip was replaced by chips that were progressively more powerful: The 8008 (1972), 8080 (1974), 8086–8088 (1978), 286 (1982), 386 (1985), and the 486 (1989).

Then in 1993, Intel marketed the first Pentium™ processor. It vastly increased the speed at which computers could process information. And it allowed the machines to process speech, sound, handwriting, and photographic images. The Pentium Pro Processor followed in 1995 and the Pentium II in 1997—both of which contained over five million transistors. The Pentium Pro processed information at 150 megahertz (Mhz) or higher and, due to a feature called Dynamic

Execution, made possible advanced 3-D visualization and interactive capabilities. The Pentium II microprocessor could process information at speeds ranging from 233 Mhz to 450 Mhz. (A megahertz is equal to 1 million hertz. A hertz is a unit of radio-wave frequency equal to one cycle per second.)

The rapid development of computer technology meant that each new computer model was soon replaced by a faster, more powerful machine. Computers in the 1970s could check eight bits of data at every hertz. (Eight bits is called a byte, and each byte contains 256 possible combinations of 1s and 0s.) The 1980s and 1990s saw the development of microprocessors that could handle 16, 32, and 64 bits of data at a time.

Developing Languages and Operating Systems

Programming computers was easier after simple computer languages called assembly languages were developed in the 1950s. Assembly languages allowed programmers to use short letter combinations to give instructions to the computer. The letter combinations stood for the 1s and 0s the machine could understand. The first commercial computer, Remington Rand's 1951 UNIVAC, and the series of IBM computers that came out in 1953 used assembly languages written specifically for them.

Working from 1954 to 1957, Grace Hopper, a computer scientist at Harvard University, invented the first general-use computer language (applicable to any computer), called FORTRAN (FORmula TRANslator). Other general-use languages followed: ALGOL (ALGOrithmic Language) in 1957; COBOL (Common Business Oriented Language); and BASIC (Beginner's All-purpose Symbolic Instruction Code) in the 1960s. Additional general-use languages that are still in use include PASCAL, LOGO for children, C, developed by Bell Laboratories in the 1970s, and LISP and PROLOG, which are used in artificial intelligence.[4]

Up to the late 1950s, computers functioned without operating systems (OSs). An operating system is a program that controls all of the machine's resources, from memory to printers and monitors. Computers without operating systems were difficult to program, since thousands of commands were needed to do one task. They were also slow to process instructions.

Then in 1956, Bob Patrick, a programmer at General Motors, and Owen Mock, an engineer from North American Aviation, developed a three-phase operating system for IBM computers. With this system, called GM–NAA I/O, the IBM 704 computer could do twenty times more work in a given period than earlier models.

By 1966 IBM had developed an operating system for its System/360 computers called OS/360. This operating system was more versatile than past programs. IBM filled a thousand orders a month for its System/360 machines in 1966. At the end of that year there were more than thirty-five thousand computers in use in the United States.[5] The number of

The IBM 650 Computer, circa 1953. This series of computers used assembly languages written especially for them.

computer users spiraled again with the 1983 release of the popular movie *War Games*. In the film a high school student nearly starts a world war when he uses a home computer to gain entry into defense department computers.[6]

By 1980 more user-friendly operating systems, such as Microsoft's Disk Operating System (MS-DOS) and the Apple Operating System, were introduced. MS-DOS let the computer keep track of files, run and link programs, and access attached devices, such as printers and disk drives.

In the late 1980s, Microsoft produced Windows 3.1, a program that masked the MS-DOS operating system. It also made computers more user-friendly by displaying options in boxes (windows) that users could select with the click of a mouse. (The Windows concept was also used early on by Apple's Macintosh computers.) In 1995, Microsoft developed the operating system Windows 95, which evolved into Windows 98.

While MS-DOS and the Windows series were developed for personal computers, more powerful mainframe computers have continued to use Unix, an operating system developed in 1969 by two researchers at American Telephone & Telegraph's (AT&T) Bell Laboratories.[7] Users can assemble the system's software tools in a variety of ways to perform specific tasks. The tools themselves can be taken apart and modified by individual users. This characteristic gives users unusual control over computer performance. By contrast, the code that drives MS-DOS or Windows 95 is locked away from users. Most network servers connected to the Internet are based on the Unix operating system, because of its adaptability and ease of use.

Personal Computers Multiply

The increasing popularity of personal computers has spurred manufacturers to produce ever faster and more powerful machines, in shorter and shorter time intervals. In 1990 an IBM survey found that consumers were replacing their personal computers every five years to keep up with new developments. By 1995 most users considered their machines obsolete in just two years. It is estimated that by the year 2005 the total number of personal computers consigned to the junk heap will have reached 150 million.[8]

Computer Basics

Regardless of size, all computers are composed of five essential parts: (1) a central processing unit (CPU); (2) input devices, such as a keyboard, mouse, stylus, light wand, voice recognition program, or other method of entering information; (3) memory storage devices; (4) output devices, such as monitors, speakers, and printers; and (5) a communications network that links all the parts of the system and can connect the system to other computers. *Hardware* refers to the physical equipment, both basic and optional, that makes up a computer system. *Software* is the term used for the instructions (programs) that make a computer perform its various functions.

The CPU is the computer's brain. It consists of one chip or several chips and it runs programs. Programs are lists of instructions (algorithms) that tell the computer how to use incoming data. A variety of input devices allow users to enter data and commands into the computer. The keyboard, patterned after the keys on a typewriter, is the most common input device. It is used to type into the computer the information needed to run a program.

Information may also be entered into the

The IBM Stretch 7030 looked like a machine from a science-fiction movie.

computer by clicking the buttons on a mouse (an attachment that lets the user choose from menus on the monitor screen). In computers with touch screens, users can choose applications by using a finger to touch choices displayed on the screen. Other input devices include light pens that allow users to draw directly on the computer monitor screen; voice recognition software that lets users speak commands into a microphone attached to the computer; and a stylus, or pen, with which users can "write" information directly on the computer screen.

The memory of the computer stores information to be processed by the CPU. Memory is measured in bytes. A kilobyte (K) actually equals about 1,024 bytes, and a megabyte (Mb) equals approximately 1,048,576 bytes. By the late 1990s, hard-drive memory was most often measured in gigabytes (GB) (giga=1 billion).

A computer has two kinds of memory. Random-access memory (RAM) is used to store and retrieve all types of information. Data stored in RAM is lost when the computer is turned off, unless the user first stores the information to disk before turning off the machine. For example, you use a word-processing program to type a letter. The letter is temporarily stored in RAM while you are writing it, but it will be lost when you turn off the computer unless you first give the command to store it to disk.

The second type of memory in a computer is called ROM, for read-only memory. ROM permanently stores information that the computer needs to operate when in use. (This information is usually installed by the computer manufacturer and cannot be changed; it can only be read.) ROM, for example, stores the first program to run when the computer is turned on. This program is called the bootstrap loader. The bootstrap loader retrieves the operating system. Unlike RAM, the data in ROM is not lost when the computer is turned off.

Memory storage units called disk drives read and write information to or from a diskette. Disk drives are housed in the system unit, which also includes the central processing unit (CPU), and various adapters and options. Disk drives are most often "floppy" or fixed. *(Floppy* is a term for a removable diskette, derived from the first disks, which were thin and flexible.) A fixed, or hard, disk is a high-speed, large-capacity disk drive. The hard disk cannot be removed from the disk drive. A fixed disk can hold much more information than the floppy, or removable, diskette. (Most mainframe computers store data on magnetic tape.)

In addition to floppy and fixed disk drives, personal computers may also have a compact disk, or CD-ROM drive. These use the same laser technology as audio compact disks (CDs). Since compact disks can contain a huge amount of data, they enable

The Pentium II microprocessor, developed by Intel Corporation in 1997, contained over five million transistors. A computer using a Pentium II can operate very quickly.

computers to play complicated video and audio programs. Output devices allow computer users to see the results of their data input. The most common output device is the monitor, or video display terminal (VDT). This is the televisionlike screen that displays information typed into the computer, and lets the user interact with the machine.

Other output devices include printers and modems. Printers are attached to computers to print out information on paper, transparency film, fabric, and other materials. Most printers today are one of two types: dot matrix or laser. Dot matrix printers contain pins that are controlled by springs and magnets. The pins strike an inked ribbon to form letters or graphic images made up of tiny inked dots. Laser printers generate and use radio frequency energy to produce a concentrated beam of light (laser beam). The laser beam creates an image made up of dots on a photosensitive drum. A powder, called toner, is applied to the drum, and sticks to the dots, forming letters and graphics. The image is then heat-set on the paper. Both types of printers are capable of printing in color, as well as in black and white.

The modem was the first equipment option that allowed PC users to communicate with other computers across telephone lines. Modems may be installed inside the system unit as special circuit cards (internal modems), or they may be connected to the computer externally (external modems). The telephone line is connected to the modem, which is, in turn, connected to the computer.

The modem (short for modulator-demodulator)

translates the computer's digital pulses (a series of 1s and 0s) to analog (continuous) sound waves, which can be transmitted over telephone lines much like the human voice. This is called modulation. The modem connected to the computer at the receiving end then translates the analog waves back to digital form (demodulation), so the computer can read the message. A special communications program is needed to run a modem. Modems are now standard equipment in personal computers.

Modem speeds are expressed in bits per second (bps). The faster the modem speed, the faster information is transmitted and received. By 1998 the speediest modems for personal computers transmitted at 56 kilobauds (56,000 bps), but 128 bps modems were in development.

Networks, the Internet, and the Web

Modems linked distant computers, creating networks. Networks made possible speedy information exchange.

Wide area networks, which require the use of satellites and cables designed to handle data transmission, allow linked computers to communicate. The world's first wide-area network, named the Arpanet for its developer (the Pentagon's Advanced Research Projects Agency), began operating in 1969. It linked computers used by researchers for the United States Department of Defense.

The Arpanet became part of a complex of networks called the Internet, developed in the mid-1980s. In the early days of the Internet, most regular users were researchers at government agencies and universities. Few "ordinary" people used the Internet for two reasons: Only a small percentage of households had personal computers, and the Internet then was difficult for novice users to navigate.

Then in 1989, Tim Berners-Lee, a scientist at the European Laboratory for Particle Physics, wrote a special programming language called hypertext markup language (html) that linked documents on the Internet. He called the project the World Wide Web, and by 1993 it was fully operational. Berners-Lee's creation made navigating the Internet so easy that by the end of 1997, Nua, an Internet strategy, research, and development agency, estimated that 100.5 million people had Internet access in their homes. By the end of the year 2000, that number will increase to 200 million. The United States Department of Commerce estimates that Internet traffic doubles every one hundred days, resulting in a yearly growth rate of more than 700 percent.[9]

Net Technology

In the 1970s Bell Telephone Labs developed technology to allow low-cost communication in data, voice, video, and graphic media over existing telephone lines. The system, called Integrated Services Digital Network (ISDN), can relay information in digital form, so that modems are not needed to send data between computers. In 1998, ISDN service was still limited to specific locations, but subscribers fortunate enough to have the service could zip large amounts of information to receiving computers in seconds, as opposed to in minutes by modem.[10]

By 1998 the race to provide speedy, affordable access to the Internet had created three new technologies: cable modems, asymmetric digital subscriber lines (ADSL), and satellite service. Cable modems transmit digital data over the same coaxial cable that brings television signals into homes. The cable is split, so that one end goes into the television set and the other plugs into the personal computer. The computer must be equipped with a small internal circuit board and a special cable modem that operates at 1 million to 2 million bits per second.

ADSL service is provided through local telephone companies. In 1998 about four thousand American computer users subscribed to ADSL, but that number was expected to quickly increase.[11] To use the service, computer users need special modems that operate at 1.5 million bits per second.[12]

Computer users may also subscribe to fast Internet service through a satellite, which provides service at about 400 kilobits per second. Users must buy a special dish and pay for its installation, plus a monthly service charge.

Computer Crime: The Early Days

Computer crime began before the Internet. According to August Bequai's *Techno-Crimes, The Computerization of Crime and Terrorism*, the first reported case of computer crime dates back to 1958, and the first federal prosecution to 1966.[13]

Donn B. Parker, author of *Crime by Computer* and *Fighting Computer Crime*, reported 374 cases of "computer abuse" from 1958 to 1976. In four of these cases, the computer was actually shot by frustrated users. Two of the four "wounded" machines were a total loss; the remaining two were dented by bullets but bravely continued to run.[14]

Computer Crime on the Rise in the 1980s and 1990s

By 1980 more individuals—many of them high school and college students—were learning the secrets of computing. And more employees had jobs in computer operations as systems administrators and analysts, programmers, data entry clerks, and service people. As a result, more people knew computer systems, thus increasing the chances the machines would be misused in illegal or unethical ways.

In the late 1980s and early 1990s, three major computer crimes gained national attention.

In 1986, Clifford Stoll, an astronomer at the University of California at Berkeley, discovered a seventy-five-cent difference in the two accounting programs that kept track of the school's computer account users. His dogged determination to find the missing seventy-five cents led to the capture of a group of German hackers who were paid by the Russian KGB to search for U.S. military secrets. (See Chapter 7.)

In 1988, Robert Tappan Morris, a twenty-three-year-old Cornell University graduate student, created and released on the Internet a program called a worm. (A *worm* is a program that reproduces itself inside a computer and spreads to other machines, but unlike a *virus* it does not rewrite data. It is, however, considered malicious.)

Morris's invader worm attacked host computers through three sets of commands. One set told the computer to copy the original program hundreds of times. A second set searched out the names of all rightful users of the system and captured their passwords. The third set told the computer to send copies of the original program to every other system it could reach.

Morris later said he created the program as an experiment, intending that it slowly and harmlessly copy itself across the networks. Instead, he made a programming mistake that caused the worm to reproduce much faster than he had planned. The destructive program soon clogged infected computers with unwanted electronic files, stopping all normal functions of the machines. Estimates of the number of machines that crashed as a result of the attack ranged from three thousand to sixty-two hundred. The Computer Virus Industry Association estimated total damage in lost work, lost user hours, and manhours required to deworm infected systems at over $98 million.[15]

In January 1990 a group of young computer users called the Masters of Deception (MOD) attacked the computers of a regional operating company of AT&T, shutting down local telephone service in parts of the Northeast.[16] This and other incidents involving stolen credit card numbers and accessing government computers eventually led to the arrests of some members of the Masters of Deception (MOD).

Present-Day Computer Crime

In the 1990s the fast growth of the Internet and the World Wide Web contributed to more computer break-ins—both benign and destructive. For example, tampering with Web sites, usually those of high-profile government agencies, allowed hackers to showcase their skills (or laugh at the establishment).

- August 17, 1996—The U.S. Justice Department's Web page became "US (Japan's) Department of Injustice Home Page," which included a rambling protest against the Communications Decency Act.

- September 19, 1996—The Central Intelligence Agency's (CIA's) Web page was mistitled the "Central Stupidity Agency."

- December 29, 1996—The U.S. Air Force's Web page was replaced with a page of aviation statistics and a pornographic photograph.[17]

- Also in 1996, at the Web site of Great Britain's Labour Party, hackers replaced the picture of Prime Minister Tony Blair with one of his *Spitting Image* puppets and titled the site "New Labour—Same Politicians. Same Lies."[18]

These pranks caused no serious damage, but they demonstrated that, without adequate security measures, linked computers are at the mercy of crackers. (*Cracker* is a term first recommended by Richard Stallman, founder of the Free Software Foundation, to distinguish between the benign deeds of "true" hackers and the activities of computer criminals.)[19] In fact, a December 1996 survey of two thousand government and commercial Web sites by security expert Dan Farmer found that over two thirds of the Web sites surveyed would be easy to crack, mostly because of mistakes or oversights in setting them up.[20]

With increasing use of the Internet in the 1990s, more serious forms of computer crime also became popular. For example, armed with a person's full name and Social Security number, electronic swindlers used Internet databases to call up an address, telephone number, employee number, or driver's license number of an unsuspecting victim. Using these stolen good names, thieves could then apply for credit. One victim of such an "identity theft"—a twenty-eight-year-old special-events planner in California—found herself billed for a new $22,000 Jeep, charges on five new credit cards, an apartment, and a $3,000 loan.[21]

Potentially more dangerous than thieves in the 1990s were those criminals who used the networks to threaten the physical safety of others. In April 1994 *USA Today* reported the following incidents:

- A 19-year-old Texas college student was

indicted for sending e-mail death threats to President Bill Clinton.

- A Massachusetts man was sentenced to twenty years in prison for using computer conversations to lure boys into face-to-face meetings, and then sexually assaulting them.

- Also in Massachusetts, a businessman pleaded innocent to charges that he operated a computer network that transmitted child pornography.[22]

Such offenses prompted federal and state law enforcement agencies to form special task forces to track cybercrime.

The Cost of Computer Crime

Business losses from computer crime have risen as use of the Internet has increased. Scott Charney, chief of the Computer Crime and Intellectual Property Section at the U.S. Department of Justice, reported that in 1991 computer fraud was costing American businesses $5 billion a year. By 1998 the cost had risen to $10 billion annually.[23]

In two studies completed in July 1998, Fortune 1000 companies reported more losses in 1997 from computer vandalism and espionage than ever before. Several companies said a single break-in cost them $10 million or more.[24]

The exact total cost of computer crime is hard to pinpoint. Many businesses and agencies do not report break-ins, because they don't want the public to know that security has been breached. In fact, a recent study by WarRoom Research LLC, a computer security consultancy based in Annapolis, Maryland, estimates that of the companies that detect system break-ins, only about 12 percent report the crime.[25]

Criminal acts in cyberspace have multiplied as the number of computer users and use of the Internet have increased, but in many cases the crimes themselves were not new. More computers and the development of the Internet simply gave computer criminals a new environment and new tools to use in plying their trade.

3

Hacking U.S.A.

The term *hacker* originated in the 1960s. It was used to describe college students at the Massachusetts Institute of Technology (MIT) who couldn't get enough of computers. Desktop computers had not yet been invented, so the students vied for time on the few mainframe computers available, writing their own programs for the machines.

Hacker was a label of pride for those early programmers. They loved to probe a system's secrets and the bigger the system the better. These hackers believed computer time, know-how, and software should be free and freely shared, and they resented those who would protect ownership. At the same time, early hackers had strict unwritten rules against erasing or damaging others' files, changing data, or using a system for personal gain.

As time passed and interest in and access to computers grew, more young persons called themselves hackers. But the meaning of the term *hacker* had gradually changed. It was once used to mean computer competence and knowledge. But the media used the term so often to describe computer criminals that it came to mean someone who breaks into computers to do damage. Hackers of the old school objected to the negative use of the term. To distinguish these hackers from their less reputable colleagues, today the term *cracker* is more often used to mean cybercriminal.

In 1998 online columnist, author, and former hacker Douglas Thomas claimed that the "elegant" hacker philosophy of the past still exists.

> Most hackers consider two things taboo: destroying information and making money off a hack. Those two things are enough to get you shunned in most hacker circles, or at least give you a very bad reputation. Hackers are often very smart computer users, but, for the most part, they make lousy criminals. Once money is involved, the chances of getting busted skyrocket. They also, I think, see money as defiling a more pure pursuit—figuring out how things work.[1]

Conflicting Opinions

But experts disagree about whether or not hackers are harmless. Willis Marti, director of Computing and

Facilities Services Group at Texas A & M University in College Station, compares hackers to house intruders:

> What would you do with someone who tried all the doors in an apartment complex, and if he found one unlocked, simply walked in to look around? Most people would take a pretty dim view of that. Most computer hacking is no different than that.[2]

Eugene Spafford, a nationally known computer security expert and a professor of computer science at Purdue University in West Lafayette, Indiana, says the argument that breaking into computer systems is harmless because it is motivated by curiosity is off base.

> Clearly that's disconnected thinking as far as how [unauthorized access] really impacts on people . . . Do all the people who do illegal, unapproved things with computer systems cause damage? The answer is yes, they cause a tremendous amount of damage, such as viruses, system break-ins, crashes, vandalism, theft of proprietary information, denial of service, and so on.[3]

Furthermore, according to most computer security experts, the excuse that breaking into systems is the only way to learn is no longer valid. "Go take classes, buy some books," suggests Spafford.

> If [computer users] want to see what is on the Internet, there are millions of Web sites and they can go to a library and find an Internet connection. They can read books and write programs. They don't have to go off and use somebody else's computer system to learn.[4]

Audrey Allen, senior computer science major at Texas A&M University, College Station, Texas. As demonstrated in the attack/defend network security course taught by Willis Marti, computer security means not only locking intruders out, but may also mean locking them in until they can be identified.

"While there are still hackers who are breaking into other people's systems," says Thomas, "I think there really isn't the need to do that anymore. Years ago if you wanted to learn about a network, you pretty much had to break into one. Now that is not the case."

Thomas continues,

With the evolution of [the operating system] Linux, anyone can now run a Unix-like system on even the most rudimentary PC, and most hackers are doing that and exploring that way. Some are setting up systems online as challenges where hacking them is permitted and encouraged.[5]

Hackers once made reputations by illegally breaking into systems, but they can now visit Web sites that encourage them to legally try to break in. Once in, they can then release signed security advisories, announcing to others that they were successful and recommending fixes for the system flaws that let them in.

Why Do Hackers Hack?

True hackers (as distinguished from crackers) characterize themselves as simply curious. "You can tell who is going to be a hacker from a very early age," says Thomas. "Hackers take things apart, usually by using tools that were designed for something else. For me, it was an old rotary telephone and a butter knife." To a hacker, the inner workings of anything electronic are more interesting than the outsides.[6]

Thomas maintains that hacking activities are now of two types: (1) *True hacks*. These take knowledge and ingenuity and usually involve sneaking into a computer system through a discovered security hole. (2) *Derivative hacks*. These acts are accomplished by means of a program or script. Such programs are written after a true hack has taken place, then are passed around on the Internet. True hacks require sophisticated computer expertise and are the most original and admirable of the two types.[7]

How Great a Threat to Computer Security Are Hackers?

In *The Hacker Crackdown: Law and Disorder on the Electronic Frontier* (1992), Bruce Sterling questioned the threat posed by young curiosity-driven hackers, as opposed to insiders—those employees in computer operations who have the opportunity to commit electronic crimes. He estimated that as few as one hundred hackers were "skilled enough to penetrate sophisticated systems and truly to worry corporate security and law enforcement." However, he, too, warned that "electronic fraud, especially telecommunication crime, is growing by leaps and bounds."[8]

In 1998 Sterling still maintained that employees had "means, motive, and opportunity" to break into systems, "whereas teenager hackers only have some of the means, and the occasional opportunity, and basically nothing in the way of motive. They just don't have enough budget or stick-to-itiveness to constitute any genuine challenge to security."[9]

Sterling contrasted hackers with crackers:

> Guys with criminal intent want money. There just aren't many ways to make easy money from penetrating security on somebody's computer system. And even if there were, it would be much more effective and profitable to drive a big truck up some dark night and physically steal all their computers. Of course, to do that you'd have to be serious about it, and that's the problem with hackers in a nutshell—they're hobbyists.[10]

In a 1998 survey of 1,600 companies in fifty countries, cosponsored by PricewaterhouseCoopers and *InformationWeek*, 73 percent of the respondents reported some security breach or corporate espionage in the past year. Threats came from the following groups, in order of frequency:

- Authorized employees (58 percent of the time)

- Unauthorized employees (24 percent)

- Former employees (13 percent)

- Computer hackers or terrorists (13 percent)

- Competitors (3 percent).

Overall, those companies selling products or services from Web sites reported more security breaches involving information loss, theft of data or trade secrets, and lost revenues.[11]

A 1997–1998 survey of 320 Fortune 1000 companies conducted by WarRoom Research LLC had slightly different results. In August 1998, WarRoom president Mark Gembicki said that earlier surveys showed that the biggest threat to corporate data came from employees. WarRoom's latest research, however, showed a marked shift. In 1998, 63 percent of the companies surveyed said that outsiders committing information espionage were the biggest threat. "We define information espionage as being a directed attempt to identify and gather proprietary data and information via [the] computer networks," said Gembicki. He emphasized that hobbyist hackers were not included in this category.[12]

Who Are the Crackers?

Before 1993 no distinction was made between hackers and crackers by most law enforcement agencies. The Federal Bureau of Investigation's profile of the typical computer intruder included these traits: Most were between eighteen and thirty-five years of age. They were bright, highly motivated, adventuresome, creative, and loved a challenge. If employed, they were the first workers on the job in the morning and the last to leave at night, and they were usually among the most trusted employees. Most were male, but increasing numbers of females were cracking because more women entered the workplace as computer specialists.

As early as 1993, however, experts who tracked computer break-ins were noticing a change. According to Harold Hendershot, supervisory special agent in computer fraud and abuse for the FBI, 1990s computer criminals were less likely to be amateurs. Instead, computer users motivated by profit were cracking professionally.[13]

Scott Charney, chief of computer crime for the U.S. Department of Justice, confirmed Hendershot's assessment. By the mid-1990s, hackers arrested for the first time were older than in the past—in their twenties and thirties—and motives were changing. "The pure hacker ethic—'We want to explore the system; we don't want to do any damage; we don't want to steal anything'—may still exist," he said. "But more and more we are seeing cases where that ethic does not exist, and there is an ulterior motive, such as profit."[14]

In 1998, Dora Winter, an information technology expert and "hacker tracker" at the University of Michigan in Ann Arbor, said she saw two distinct groups of computer intruders: young males between the ages of eighteen and twenty-three who were more likely to commit electronic practical jokes than to do data damage or steal; and a second group of middle-aged individuals—also most often male—with technical know-how, who broke into computer systems to steal or destroy information. (A few females were investigated for computer trespass, but both groups were mostly male.) According to Winter, members of the older group of crackers tended to be disgruntled employees seeking revenge for perceived slights, or were trespassing electronically for personal gain.

Winter also distinguished between hackers of the old school and the hacker subculture, where such acts as posting stolen software or pilfered credit card numbers were most likely to occur. "The two groups aren't the same," Winter emphasized, "and they don't necessarily get along. We refer to hackers as persons who like to play with code, to try to get it to do something it wasn't intended to do. It's not a derogatory term used to mean breaking into computer systems."[15]

In Paul Taylor's 1996 book, *Hackers*, Chris Goggans, a.k.a. Erik Bloodaxe, former leader of the hacker group Legion of Doom, and now an information security consultant, contrasted attitudes among members of today's hacker underground with attitudes in the past:

> [In the early days] people were friendly, computer users were very social. Information was handed down freely, there was a true feeling of brotherhood in the underground. As the years went on people became more and more antisocial.
>
> . . . the social feeling of the underground began to vanish. People began to hoard information and turn people in for revenge. The underground today is not fun. It is very power hungry, almost feral in its actions. People are grouped off: you like me or

Dora Winter, an experienced "hacker tracker" at the University of Michigan in Ann Arbor, knows the difference between hackers and crackers.

you like him, you cannot like both. . . . The subculture I grew up with, learned in, contributed to, has decayed into something gross and twisted that I shamefully admit connection with. Everything changes and everything dies, and I am certain that within ten years there will be no such thing as a computer underground. I'm glad I saw it in its prime.[16]

Some experts maintain that the media have sensationalized hacker deeds. They say that hackers are not a serious threat to computer security because others with computer access are more apt to commit criminal or malicious acts of intrusion. Others claim that any act of computer trespass—whether by hackers who plead curiosity or by others with suspicious motives—can have unforeseen consequences that pose serious threats to personal and national security.

Clearly, such computer trespassing acts as stealing money or identities, and damaging or destroying financial or medical data are criminal. And these crimes are, of course, subject to strict legal penalties.

4

Stealing Money

In 1994, twenty-six-year-old Vladimir Levin of St. Petersburg, Russia, schemed to steal $10 million from Citibank, then the largest bank in the United States. Levin, known online as "Vova," penetrated Citibank's computer system using an obsolete 286 computer. Once in, he intercepted electronic money transfers, arranging for large sums of money to be sent to accounts he had set up in various locations. Levin planned to send others to collect the stolen money.

Meanwhile, Citibank detected the break-in and called the FBI. Federal agents tracked Levin's electronic footprints, and

53

the criminal was caught in the act. Levin pleaded guilty and, in April 1998, a New York court sentenced him to thirty-six months in prison.[1] Citibank eventually recovered all but $400,000 of the stolen money. After the theft, Citibank enacted encryption and password policies to prevent such a crime from happening again.

When the motive for a computer crime is profit, the stakes can be high. A 1998 report for Democratic members of the U.S. House Banking Committee estimated that American financial services lose a hefty $2.4 billion a year to cyberthieves.[2]

Who Are Today's Techno-Bandits?

Those who use computers to steal for profit generally fall into one of four groups:

- current or former computer operations employees;

- outsiders with technical knowledge who illegally access computer systems to commit industrial or information espionage;

- career criminals who use computers to ply their trade; and

- the cracker, as discussed in Chapter 3.

Employees and ex-employees are usually in the best position to steal from their employers, simply because they have the means, opportunity, and motive.

In 1994, Ivey James Lay was a switch engineer for the MCI telephone company in Charlotte, North

Carolina. Lay was also a hacker, known online as "Knightshadow." But he crossed the line from hacker to cracker when he wrote a program that could divert and store calling-card numbers taken from carriers using MCI's switching equipment, including AT&T, Sprint, and a number of local telephone companies. Lay sold the stolen numbers to crackers in the United States and Europe, who could then use them to make "free" long-distance telephone calls. Those whose cards were stolen were billed for the calls.

MCI officials called the case the largest of its kind in known losses. Lay was arrested and charged with stealing more than 100,000 calling-card numbers, which were used to make $50 million in long-distance calls. The telephone companies involved did not bill customers who were victimized.[3]

Another computer-employee heist, dubbed one of the biggest breaches of security of personal data held by the federal government, involved several workers at the U.S. Social Security Administration. In 1996 the government employees, based in New York and Louisiana, were paid by a ring of credit card thieves to use clients' Social Security numbers to search data files for mothers' maiden names. These names could then be used by the thieves to activate credit cards stolen from the mail. (Many banks that mail credit cards to customers require them to activate the new cards by calling a special telephone number and giving their mothers' maiden names.)

The worker arrested in the case admitted to authorities that she had checked thirty records a day for her accomplices. According to the government, early losses in unauthorized credit card charges amounted to more than \$330,000, but the final total was expected to be much higher.[4]

Career Criminals

To illustrate how familiar career criminals had become with computers, the U.S. Department of Justice's Scott Charney said in March 1995 that "in the old days," when making a drug bust, law enforcement officers would often find "white powder and currency and a little black book," containing records of illegal transactions. Today, Charney said, "you kick in the door and you find the powder and the currency and a stand-alone PC."[5]

When career criminals use computers, they can often increase their take in a big way. In New York City in the 1990s, for example, organized crime groups discovered the profit in telecommunications fraud. In one plan, the mob victimized corporations by using their private branch exchanges (PBXs) to make unauthorized telephone calls. Using computers, calls were routed from the outside, through a company's switchboard to foreign countries. The criminals sold the calls, raking in thousands of dollars each month. "These operations have become very organized very rapidly," New York State Police Senior Investigator Donald Delaney said on a radio talk show in 1992.

> I have arrested people that have printed revenue goals for the current month, next six months, and entire year—just like any other franchise operation.

At least one independent telecommunications fraud operator may have been murdered when he infringed on mob territory.[6]

Computer Theft Victims

Banks and brokerage houses are major targets of techno-thieves, because of their reliance on electronic funds transfer (EFT). According to the market research firm International Data Corporation, $117 billion in financial transactions will have taken place online by the year 2000.[7] The money transferred from bank to bank, or from payers' accounts to payees' accounts, is moved by messages passed between computers. Following coded instructions, a computer in the sending location subtracts the amount to be transferred from the appropriate account, and a computer in the receiving location adds the transferred amount to the designated account.

At either end of these financial transactions, if the coded computer instructions are accidentally garbled—through human error or telephone equipment breakdown—or if they are deliberately changed, the transaction can go haywire. The wrong amount or no amount may be sent. The wrong account may be shorted, or the wrong one credited. Or, as in the following case, phony accounts may be established by dishonest computer users and nonexistent "deposits" credited to the account.

A proof operator at the Zions First National Bank of Utah was one of several employees responsible for balancing customer checking and savings accounts by computer. When accounts failed to balance one month, a "cash-in" debit of $3,970.40 was discovered. An investigation revealed that a savings account had been opened in the name of "Mark Weaver" and credited with $3,970.40. Most of the money was withdrawn soon after, as $2,000 in cash and a cashier's check for $1,300. Investigators could find no record of a "Mark Weaver," and the address given for him did not exist. The proof operator was arrested on embezzlement charges when she bragged to a coworker about her scheme.[8]

The practice of keeping track of money online has led to other types of illegal financial antics:

- *Lapping.* An employee diverts incoming cash to a bogus account. He or she immediately replaces the stolen money with more incoming cash. Employers can prevent lapping by making sure the same employee who handles cash is not also recording transactions.

- *Kiting.* Normal delays in processing financial transactions are used to create the appearance of assets where assets do not exist. Kiting is prevented when financial institutions allow time for transactions to be completed before releasing funds. For example, bank deposits made by check should be allowed to clear the payer's bank and appear as interbank transfers before the customer is allowed access to the funds.

- *Money laundering.* Illegal profits, such as money made selling drugs, are routed through legitimate business accounts to make them appear legal.

Automatic teller machines are also popular targets for thieves. According to *Forbes* magazine, personal-identification-number (PIN)-related ATM fraud accounts for $100 million to $200 million in annual losses.[9]

The handy ATMs, located in bank lobbies and drive-up lanes, and in many restaurants, stores, and shopping malls, allow account holders to withdraw or deposit money using coded plastic cards. After inserting the card, users type in a PIN, then indicate which transaction they want.

In one ATM scam, crooks in Miami, Florida, put plastic sleeves into the card slots of an ATM. Then when the machine grabbed the card of a user and refused to let go, the customer reached for the nearby telephone and dialed the conveniently posted customer service number. Instead of a legitimate customer service representative, however, the telephone, provided by the thieves, was also manned by them. The bogus representative asked each frustrated card user for his or her PIN, promising that a replacement card would be mailed out in a few days. The thieves then used tweezers to remove the "stuck" ATM cards.[10]

ATM fraud took a new twist when, in the mid-1990s, banks began issuing ATM cards that doubled as debit cards. The cards could be used to withdraw cash from ATMs, using a PIN in the usual manner, or to pay for purchases in stores without using the PIN.

When used to buy merchandise, the amount of the purchase was immediately deducted from the customer's checking account. A 1996 article in *Forbes* magazine warned readers that the new cards "could give a thief carte blanche to your checking account." Since there was no credit float, or withhold-payment option, as with credit cards, "your bank balance and credit line could be depleted, and your checks could be bouncing all over town."[11] In fact, losses reported by Visa and MasterCard debit card issuers for 1995 totaled $19 million.[12]

In some cases, entire ATMs have been stolen and pilfered, but most often, stolen or lost magnetic cards and PINs are used to raid ATM accounts. Sometimes thieves steal PINs simply by *piggybacking* or *shoulder-surfing*—looking over the shoulders of legitimate customers while they are using the machines. They then enter the stolen numbers and withdraw money from victims' accounts.

The same method may be used to filch the codes from users of telephone calling cards. Senior Investigator Delaney of the New York State Police remarked,

> If you go into the Port Authority Bus Terminal and look up in the balcony, you will see rows of people 'shoulder-surfing' with binoculars . . . or telescopes trained on the public telephones. When they see a person making a credit card call, they repeat the numbers into a tape recorder [or it is relayed to an accomplice's beeper]. The number is then sold and, within a few days, it is in use all around the city.[13]

Personal Identification Numbers can be stolen by "shoulder-surfing"—looking over the shoulder of a customer using an automatic teller machine.

By 1996 one of the fastest growing theft-by-computer rackets was check fraud. A couple of thousand dollars in personal computers, plus color copiers or scanners, could quickly set thieves up in business. "Bank robberies and ATM fraud are a drop in the bucket compared to check fraud," said a security expert for Texas Commerce Bank. "This is an attractive [criminal] area because the risks are low and the rewards are great."[14]

In most states the crooks duplicated and forged payroll checks from well-known area companies. Thumbprint recognition was used by some banks to thwart the thieves. This proved less successful, however, than *account reconciliation*. Through this method, the program's corporate subscribers sent via computer to the bank the number and amount of any checks written. The bank could then immediately reconcile checks written against charges received to a subscriber's account. If checks were submitted for payment that did not appear on the subscriber's list, they could be traced.

Data Diddling, Salami Slicing, and Blackmail

Honest mistakes sometimes happen, as in 1992 when a few minutes before closing time at Salomon Brothers, Inc., a clerk hit the wrong key on a stock trading computer. A sell order was mistakenly sent for an estimated $500 million in fifty major stocks on the New York Stock Exchange. In minutes the Dow Jones Industrial Average dropped nearly twelve points.[15]

In many cases involving EFT and other electronic communications, however, the coded messages that make the computer transaction possible have been deliberately changed by someone who knows the system.

Changing data going into a computer or during output from a computer is called *data diddling*. For example, criminals have inserted registration for ships that do not exist on the computers of maritime insurance agencies. After buying policies for huge amounts, the cyberpirates "sink" them by again falsifying computer data. They then file claims to recover damages.[16]

The Internet has provided increased opportunities for data diddling. Swindlers set up phony Web sites, for instance, or they tinker with the data on Web sites, in order to intercept e-mailed orders for legitimate companies. Fronted by exact duplicates of corporate logos and offerings, the sites dupe customers into "buying" products that are never delivered. Since purchases via Web sites are made with credit cards, thieves can score twice—once by collecting fees for merchandise that is never delivered, and again by stealing credit card numbers. Such false-front Web sites have included a computer retailer, a well-known catalogue company, and one that offered to deliver a buyer's FBI report in forty-eight hours.[17]

Salami slicing is a form of data diddling that occurs when an employee steals small amounts from a large number of sources through the electronic changing of data (like slicing thin pieces from a roll of salami). Several variations of salami slicing have been used by techno-bandits. Take, for example, the greedy computer programmers employed by a New York garment-making company. They told the company's computer to increase by two cents the withholding for federal income taxes from each of their fellow employees' weekly paycheck. Each two-cent overcharge was electronically transferred into the programmers' withholding accounts. At tax time at the end of the year, the programmers received a large refund check from the Internal Revenue Service.[18]

Sometimes knowledgeable computer users use extortion to force a company to pay ransom. They plant destructive programs, then threaten to set them off if money is not paid, or they hold stolen programs or files hostage until the company pays up. In June 1996 the London *Times* reported that banks and investment firms in Great Britain and the United States had "secretly paid ransom to prevent costly computer meltdown and a collapse in confidence among their customers." The article claimed that victims, who did not report the blackmail, had paid as much as £13 million per incident to cyberterrorists based in America and Russia.[19]

Money is stolen online by thieves using computers, but the information stored in computers, and the actual online time used, also are valuable.

5

Information Profiteers

John Draper, a.k.a. "Cap'n Crunch," earned his alias when he discovered that the whistle that came in Cap'n Crunch cereal was a perfect match for the 2600-hertz tone used by the telephone company's switching system. He found that the whistle's tone could be used to trick the system into granting free access to long-distance lines.

Draper was reportedly the first *phone phreak* (a hacker who specializes in cracking telephone systems) who could bounce a call around the world, then back to himself. After he was featured in an article about hackers and phreaks in a 1971 issue of *Esquire*, Draper's telephone was tapped by the FBI. In 1972 he was caught making an illegal call to Australia. He pleaded guilty to wire fraud and was fined one thousand dollars, and sentenced to five years' probation. Draper later made more illegal calls and served four months in prison.

After his release from prison, Draper wrote an automatic dialing program for phreaking. When he put it into use, he was caught and arrested again. He pleaded guilty to wire fraud once more and was sentenced to another year in jail.[1]

When he finished this prison term, Draper was not arrested again.

Phone Phreaks

The first hackers, even before those at MIT, were phone phreaks. In fact, breaking into telephone systems goes back almost as far as Alexander Graham Bell's invention of the telephone in 1876. Bruce Sterling claims in *The Hacker Crackdown* that the first teenage males were "flung off" the new telephone system by enraged authorities as early as 1878.[2]

Before computers with modems, phone phreaks pioneered the *blue box*—a gadget that mimicked the phone switching system's 2600-hertz tone, which signaled the equipment to release circuits. By holding the blue box up to a telephone receiver, users could call any long-distance number without a toll charge.

Throughout the 1960s and into the 1970s, selling blue boxes was a source of spending money for many electronically savvy college students. Steven

Jobs and Steve Wozniak, founders of Apple Computer, sold homemade blue boxes in their under-graduate days—absolutely guaranteed—at the low price of eighty dollars each.[3]

Telephone companies have been popular victims of intruders for two reasons. First, they have always used the most powerful computers available, and this was a lure for any hacker itching to learn through practice. And second, many hackers justified their crimes against telephone companies by characterizing them as cold, greedy bureaucracies.

In the mid-1970s, AT&T reported losing an esti-mated $30 million a year to telephone fraud.[4] In 1998, precise figures on losses were not available, but estimates were that long-distance fraud cost between $4 billion and $8 billion annually. All forms of telecommunications fraud cost as much as $10 billion to $15 billion yearly,[5] and wireless fraud alone had passed the $1 billion mark.[6]

Wireless Phreaking

Wireless fraud took many forms in the 1990s, but one of the most popular was the theft of cellular phone codes and *cloning*. Thieves produced exact duplicates, or clones, of cell phones by using mail-order scanners to steal from the air the transmitter codes for analog cellular phones. The stolen codes were then used to program computer chips, which were placed inside the clones. Victims received bills for hundreds or even thousands of dollars' worth of calls they had not made. Cities hardest hit, because of high concentrations of drug traffickers, included Los Angeles, Miami, Detroit, Houston, Nashville, and New York City.

The practice was so prevalent in New York City that in 1994 even the city's mayor, police commissioner, and a city council member were victims of cloners.[7] Carriers try to prevent cloning by using many preventive measures, including assigning customer PINs for making calls.

Other Forms of Telecommunications Fraud

Some of the more common forms of telecommunication theft include:

- *Private branch-exchange (PBX) fraud.* Crackers take advantage of a PBX feature that allows company employees to dial into the home office—usually on an 800 line—from outside. After punching in a PIN, employees can make calls as if they were at work. This allows the company to save long-distance telephone charges. Once they learn a company's 800 number, crackers dial that number, then use redial programs to crack PINs and dial back out. The company is then billed as the source of the call.

- *Subscriber fraud.* Thieves simply use a phony identity to sign up for cellular telephone or regular telephone service.

- *Toll-free fraud.* Crooks route billable long-distance telephone calls through a company's toll-free 800 or 888 number by calling a toll-free number, then hacking around the phone system until they are connected to an outside line. The scam only works if the 800 number is answered by a computer, not a person.

- *Modem fraud.* A cracker calls a computer network and gains access to its local area network, which is then used to make free long-distance calls.

Stealing Credit Information

Visa and MasterCard both claimed in 1997 that losses to fraud were down from previous years. But Visa still reported $490 million lost to fraud in 1997. In mid-1998, MasterCard had not released figures.[8]

Crackers who steal credit card numbers for resale or personal use are called *carders*.

By the 1990s credit-reporting agencies had become frequent carder victims. In May 1997 a carder code-named Smak arranged online to sell a CD-ROM encrypted with 100,000 stolen credit card numbers. Smak and a mobster were to meet at the San Francisco International Airport to make the exchange. Smak didn't know, however, that the "mobster" he had been e-mailing was an FBI agent. When Smak (a thirty-six-year-old man from Daly City, California) showed up to exchange his CD for the money, he was arrested.

In June 1997 Smak was indicted on three counts of computer crime and two counts of trafficking in stolen credit cards. He pleaded guilty on four counts. Visa's fraud control team said Smak had compromised 86,326 credit card accounts, affecting 1,214 financial institutions. Potential loss was estimated at $1 billion. At $125 per card, simply reissuing the compromised cards would have cost $10 million.[9]

By 1998 trading stolen credit card numbers over the Internet had become a favorite pastime for carders. The biggest problem was not that credit card numbers were being stolen from customers buying online. It was that stolen card numbers were used to *purchase* goods and services online.

Some Web merchants were so hard hit by carders that their businesses nearly failed. For example, ShellServer, a small company started in November 1997, sold accounts and services for Internet Relay Chat users. Since ShellServer's software was used by carders, the company was especially vulnerable. ShellServer received 1,400 orders in one three-month period, but because so many of the credit card numbers used were stolen, the company only approved 270. By February 1998 that number was down to ninety-five.[10]

According to John Pettitt, chief technology officer at CyberSource in 1998, carders usually belong to one of two groups: They are fourteen- to eighteen-year-old males who want to check out pornography sites, or they are older professional thieves, dealing in high-priced items they can easily fence, such as notebook computers and printers. To protect his own company from mounting losses to carders, Pettitt developed software called IVS Fraud Screen, which allows merchants to check identities of online charge customers.[11]

Social Engineering and Dumpster Diving

Many phone phreaks, including John Draper and Kevin Mitnick, got the technical information they needed from telephone companies simply by calling and asking for it. They used facts they had already learned to convince the person on the other end of the telephone that they were employees and therefore entitled to the information they requested. The technique is called *social engineering*.

In one of the more notorious incidents of social engineering, a young man in California posed as a magazine writer to gain entry to a telephone company, where helpful employees answered his questions about the parts distribution system. He then used his computer to order parts and have them delivered to spots where he could easily pick them up. Before he was caught, he had started his own telephone equipment supply business, employing ten people. He reportedly settled a civil law suit for $8,500.[12]

"Dumpster diving" or "trashing" is another way to get company documents, credit card and telephone charge card numbers, and other restricted information. A person simply searches wastebaskets when left alone in an office, or visits the victim's garbage dump after hours to sift through the day's trash. In other words, the "trasher" hunts for information that a victim, never thinking it would be retrieved and used by someone else, has discarded.

Bulletin Boards, Web Sites, and Hacker Groups

Stolen information is often shared or listed for sale by posting it on bulletin-board systems (BBSs), on Web pages, or in newsgroups or chat rooms. Before the Web, bulletin boards were the most popular means of online information exchange. A BBS consists of a computer system, telecommunications software, a telephone line, and a modem. The first computer bulletin board for PCs was started in 1978, and by the early 1990s there were over 40,000 BBSs in the United States.[13]

Large bulletin boards are operated as commercial services available to the public. There are also thousands of smaller, privately owned BBSs. Some bulletin boards use passwords and have rules that callers must follow or risk being booted from the system. Others have no rules at all.

Hackers and crackers have their own bulletin boards, Web sites, and newsgroups. In addition, many online magazines and mailing lists are published for them. For example, *Phrack*, *2600*, *Wired*, and *The Computer Underground Digest* are magazines that exist primarily for hacker-readers. "Bugtraq," "Cypherpunks," "Sneakers," and "Tiger" are three examples of the many online mailing lists available for hackers. While some of the more infamous hacker groups, such as Masters of Deception and the Legion of Doom, have faded from the scene, others still exist—usually at specific Web sites or newsgroups online. Here are a few examples: The Cult of the

Dead Cow, Computer Underground Society, 8lgm (Eight Little Green Men), Internet Liberation Front, Spur of the Moment Elite Social Club (SOtMESC), The Inner Circle, Anarchist Hacking Klan, M2Fusion, X-ploit (a group based in Mexico), Hacker's Club, Hack the Nation, Cosmos, Illuminati, and Eden Matrix.

Arresting the Culprits

Police across the country sometimes run their own bulletin boards, trapping unwary crackers who use the service to post stolen information or to brag about exploits. For instance, in 1995 an undercover Secret Service special agent operated a bulletin-board system called "Celco 51" based in Bergen County, New Jersey. By monitoring the system, he snared crackers in seven states who were using the BBS to deal in stolen cellular telephone and credit card numbers.[14]

To keep up with cybercriminals, law enforcement agencies have had to play catch-up. The FBI and the U.S. Department of Justice have established computer crime squads. The FBI has also set up computer criminal squads in several major cities, including New York City, San Francisco, Boston, Chicago, Dallas, and Los Angeles. Many state and city law enforcement departments also have squads of officers specially trained in tracking computer criminals and in collecting technical evidence that will hold up in court.

6

Pranksters and Pirates

From 1996 to 1998, international Internet service provider America Online (AOL) received a series of taunting messages left by hackers who penetrated security systems. On August 21, 1998, for example, on an AOL page featuring baseball player Mark McGwire, hackers changed text so that visitors accessing the keyword "Fans" read "Mark McGwire reached fifty-one homers, that's quite a feat. I'd say that ballpark has better security than AOL." Three hackers signed their work: "Hex, TBB and Spin knock AOL out of the park!"[1]

Kevin Poulsen, a phone phreak and cracker who eventually served nearly five years in prison, often rerouted calls for directory assistance to the telephone in his bedroom. Poulsen told callers that he could not give out numbers. He said he could only direct them to the page in the telephone directory where the listing they wanted appeared.[2]

Such pranks sometimes seem funny to outside observers, but law enforcement officials take them seriously because of the potential for harm. Imagine dialing 911 to report a medical emergency, only to be connected to a phone-sex service. Hackers have boasted that such a stunt is possible.

War Games

The 1983 movie *War Games* inspired many computer buffs, and its popularity led to much editorializing about hackers. Could one teenager plunge the country into a war? Was hacking a serious threat or simply a minor annoyance blown out of proportion by one Hollywood production? Should hackers be punished as criminals? If so, how stiff should penalties be?

The fascination with breaking into military computers continues today. In 1998, an Israeli man was arrested for intrusions into United States military computer systems. Computer experts at the Pentagon were concerned, because at the time the United States was moving planes and bombs into the Persian Gulf area for a possible raid on Iraq. As part of this investigation, code-named "Solar Sunrise," agents also tracked two American teenagers who appeared to be working with the Israeli cracker.[3]

In July 1998 two sixteen-year-old boys, known

online as Makaveli and TooShort, pleaded guilty to charges they hacked into at least eleven United States government computer systems. They installed "sniffer" programs to capture passwords, inserted "trapdoor" programs to allow themselves a means to sneak in and out, and erased files to cover their tracks. (*Sniffer* programs are used by hackers to get specific information, such as user passwords, from host computers. *Trapdoor* programs create a hole through which intruders can reenter the system.) Deputy Defense Secretary John Hamre told reporters the attack on government computers was "the most organized and systematic attack the Pentagon has seen to date."[4] The boys were placed on probation and were forbidden to own a modem. Each would be allowed to access a remote computer system only under the supervision of a teacher, librarian, or employer.[5]

The Pentagon takes an estimated 250,000 hits a year from crackers. Yet attacks on federal government computers, including those at the Pentagon, are detected only 10 percent of the time. About five hundred attacks every year are considered "serious." For instance, government computer experts have found *logic bombs*—destructive code that lies dormant until activated by a programmed signal—in various agency computers. Some, they claim, may have been placed by foreign agents.[6]

Software Piracy

Stealing information in the form of software is also illegal. It is legal for bulletin boards and user groups to offer members shareware or public domain software, but making copies of commercial software for resale or to give to others is a crime. Making one backup copy of purchased software is recommended, but additional copies are illegal without the permission of the software publisher. It is also illegal for companies, schools, or other organizations to buy one copy of a program, then make additional copies for use in all their computers.

Software is covered by the 1980 Computer Software Copyright Act. In addition, a 1992 act

The Federal Bureau of Investigation (building shown above) and the U.S. Secret Service jointly investigate and enforce federal computer crime laws. In some federal cases, the Customs Department, Commerce Department, or the military may have jurisdiction.

made commercial software piracy a felony. And in 1997, Congress passed the No Electronic Theft (NET) Act, which criminalized copyright infringement even when no profit was involved.

Despite the laws against it, software piracy has increased. The Software Publishers Association (SPA) estimated that bootlegging results in a loss of $2.3 billion to American software publishers each year.[7]

In April 1997, David McCandless, writing for *Wired* magazine, interviewed online several members of the Inner Circle. Most were over thirty (the youngest was twenty-three), and most were white male professionals, some with families. All of them were experts at cracking expensive new software for uploading onto the Internet, where anyone could download it for free. The Inner Circle crackers protested that they pirated not to make a living, but simply because they could. "No money ever exchanges hands in our forum," California Red told McCandless. But, of course, the software manufacturing and marketing industry lost money for each program the "warez" crackers pirated.[8] (*Warez* is software that is electronically stolen, then distributed free over the Internet.)

By 1997 the pirating of copyrighted popular music had also become a serious problem, partly due to the powerful networked computers on university campuses and an ever-increasing population of music-loving students. Recordings by popular artists, such as Aerosmith, U2, and Alanis Morissette, were converted to digital form and uploaded to Web sites and Usenet groups, where they could be downloaded for free. The problem was publicized in January 1998 when the first lawsuit was brought by the Recording Industry Association of America against three alleged cyberspace music pirates. Plaintiffs agreed to damages of over $1 million each, but the defendants would not have to pay as long as they kept promises never to pirate again.[9]

High-tech pranks, military cracking, and software piracy may seem clever and daring at first glance. But whenever a hacker slips over the line and changes electronically stored data belonging to someone else, roams through government computers, or steals intellectual property created by someone else, that person risks legal prosecution.

7

Darkside Hacking

Kevin Lee Poulsen was born in California in 1965. At thirteen, he was obsessed with the telephone company computer system. Through Dumpster diving, social engineering, and studying company technical manuals, Poulsen learned the Pacific Bell system. On his sixteenth birthday he got a TRS 80 Radio Shack computer with a modem. Poulsen then discovered hacker bulletin boards, logging on as "Dark Dante." In 1983 he saw the movie *War Games*, and like other youngsters he was fascinated by the hacking feats portrayed.

By seventeen, Poulsen knew hacking well enough to access computers at the

University of California at Berkeley, Lawrence Livermore Labs, Los Alamos, White Sands, the Ballistics Research Lab, and a Chesapeake Bay army base. These break-ins captured the attention of law enforcement authorities, but Poulsen had yet to be prosecuted. He dropped out of high school and was refused admission to a technical school because he lacked a high school diploma. Eventually Poulsen was hired as a programmer by SRI, a Silicon Valley defense contractor.

By 1989, when Poulsen was twenty-four, he had been fired for his continuing obsession with telephone company computers. Law enforcement agents were hot on his trail. When a friend was arrested, Poulsen went on the run to avoid a similar fate. To support himself while in hiding, Poulsen and two friends devised ways to beat radio station giveaway contests. They "won" $22,000 in cash, at least two trips to Hawaii, and two $50,000 Porsches.

Now Poulsen was wanted by the FBI. According to federal authorities, he had compromised national security wiretaps, cracked military computers, committed computer fraud, and wiretapped the telephones of private citizens—including the phone of movie star Molly Ringwald.

The authorities finally arrested Poulsen on June 21, 1991. When the government agreed to drop espionage charges against Poulsen, he pleaded guilty to computer fraud, interception of wire communications, mail fraud, money laundering, and obstruction of justice. He was sentenced to fifty-one months in prison.

Poulsen was released from prison on June 4, 1996, after serving nearly five years. As part of his three-year probation, Poulsen was forbidden all access to computers and could not surf the Internet until 1999. Jonathan Littman, author of *The Watchman: The Twisted Life and Crimes of Serial Hacker Kevin Poulsen* (1997), said Poulsen claimed the "hacker ethic" had "dictated his every act." However, Littman added, ". . . he seemed to have broken his own code."[1]

Intentional Damage

Those dubbed "darkside hackers" seem drawn to computing as a means to do harm. In a 1989 case that apparently involved both profit and malice, a phone phreak who called herself "Electra" cracked the voice mail system of a hospital. Once in, she changed the passwords for voice mail accounts, giving them to fellow phreakers. Because of her activities, hospital employees were frequently unable to use the voice mail system. Electra was convicted of two counts of theft of services and two counts of unlawful use of computers.[2]

Access to computer data is often used by darkside hackers for revenge. On Thanksgiving weekend in 1995, Joshua Quittner and his wife, Michelle Slatalla, were relaxing at their home in Long Island, New York. The two had just published a book about hackers, *Masters of Deception: The Gang That Ruled Cyberspace*. Suddenly the journalists realized that their phone had not rung all weekend. When a

When crackers hack their way into computer systems of hospitals or other medical facilities, they endanger more than just the computers.

neighbor complained about a strange message on their answering machine, they realized they had been hacked. Their telephone had been reprogrammed to forward all incoming calls to another number, where callers heard a recorded message full of obscenities.[3]

Quittner and Slatalla were hit repeatedly for the next six months. They were forced to request one unlisted telephone number after another, until the crackers finally tired of the harassment.[4]

Revenge is also a powerful motive for computer employees with a grudge. In a case to be tried in 1999, a computer programmer committed the largest act of worker-related computer sabotage so far. Timothy Lloyd was hired by Omega Engineering in 1985 and fired in July 1996. Three weeks later, according to the U.S. Attorney's office in New Jersey, critical company software was deleted by a logic bomb planted by Lloyd. As a result, Omega Engineering claimed to have lost up to $10 million in sales.[5]

Malicious E-mail

Disgruntled employees may also misuse electronic mail. A former investment banker was arrested in July 1998 for allegedly using e-mail messages to harass executives of the company that fired him. For more than eighteen months after he was dismissed, the banker posted phony Internet messages in the names of company officials. One asked that readers contact a chief executive officer (using the executive's name) to console a dying child. Another, posted in the name of a vice-chairman, offered money for baby photos for a nonexistent children's book and gave the name of the executive's wife, their home address, and their telephone number.[6]

While sending malicious e-mail messages seems easy, security experts remind senders that they can often be traced. Message headers and connection logs leave electronic "footprints" even when the sender has taken pains to hide the trail.

Electronic mail has also been used by at least one cyber-businessperson to knock out the competition. In December 1997, Eugene Kashpureff, founder of an Internet company called AlterNIC, was extradited to the United States from Canada. The FBI alleged that Kashpureff had rerouted to his Web site Internet traffic intended for a competing business. Network Solutions, the rival company, claimed Kashpureff's actions cost them hundreds of thousands of dollars in business. They sued Kashpureff in civil court, but the FBI claimed that his action was also criminal computer and wire fraud.[7]

Unintentional Damage

Even those hackers who claim not to be willfully destructive can risk doing damage to get what they want, according to Gail Thackeray, a Phoenix prosecutor who specialized in computer crimes. "They'll say the true hacker never damages the system he's messing with, but he's willing to risk it."[8]

For instance, when hackers erase data files to cover their tracks after a break-in, they can do unexpected damage that they cannot repair. In an interview with a *New York Times* reporter after being caught by the FBI, a member of a group of Wisconsin teenagers who called themselves the 414s (after their local telephone area code) admitted to incorrectly erasing a file in a computer at the Sloan-Kettering Cancer Center in New York. This incident was particularly frightening because radiation therapy exposure times and dosages for cancer patients undergoing X–ray therapy were among the files kept on the center's computer.[9]

Electronic Spies

Espionage is another destructive venture that may appeal to darkside hackers. A famous case of computer espionage is detailed in *The Cuckoo's Egg*, by Clifford Stoll. In 1986, Stoll was an astrophysicist/computer expert working as a systems administrator for Lawrence Berkeley Laboratory in California. When computer account records showed a seventy-five cent discrepancy, Stoll discovered that a network intruder had been using the account of a scientist who had left the laboratory.

After several months, Stoll was able to trace the break-ins to a group of West German crackers called Chaos. The group broke into computers on the Internet, stealing military data and selling it to the Soviet KGB. Peter Carl, Markus Hess, and Dirk-Otto Brzezinski were finally indicted on espionage charges. Robert Anton Wilson, a fourth suspect, died mysteriously before he could be arrested.

The case came to trial in January 1990. Carl was sentenced to two years in prison and fined 3,000 marks ($1,500). Hess was sentenced to one year eight months and fined 10,000 marks. Brzezinski received a sentence of one year two months and a 5,000-mark fine.[10]

In 1998 a group called "The Masters of

Enter Network Password	? X

Enter your network password for Microsoft Networking.

OK

Cancel

User name: frankmac

Password: xxxxxxxx

Domain: cyberland

Frequently changing passwords makes it harder for hackers to gain access to someone else's computer.

Down-loading/2016216" claimed to have broken into the Pentagon's telecommunications system. Reportedly, they stole software for a military satellite system and threatened to sell it to terrorists. The Pentagon expressed concern that the group had compromised the safety of the satellite Global Positioning System.[11]

Cyberspace Predators

Among the most disturbing darkside computer users are those who surf the Internet solely to prey on innocent victims. These individuals may have no special computer expertise. They use the technology as simply another way to harass or stalk their prey. Newspapers contain many examples:

- A man "meets" a schoolteacher through e-mail, then asks her to meet him face-to-face.

The meeting convinces the teacher that she wants nothing to do with the man, but he relentlessly pursues her through e-mail and telephone messages. He is charged with stalking and faces up to a year in jail and a $1,000 fine.

- A man exchanges e-mail with a child, then lures the child to his apartment and sexually assaults him.

- A college student posts on the Internet a rape/torture/murder fantasy that uses the name of a female classmate. The "fantasy" is so realistic that the student is arrested and suspended from school. (He is not prosecuted, because of First Amendment rights.)

Parents and children should heed the dangers, said University of California-Los Angeles constitutional law professor Eugene Volokh in commenting on the above cases. But they should not be afraid to learn the new technology. "It would be much better for a parent to tell a kid that there are nasty people out there who may want to talk to you, and if they want to meet you, you should talk to me first because they may . . . be bad."[12]

Darkside hackers are determined to use their skills in ways meant to cause the most harm. Because of the damage such acts can do, the antisocial and criminal behavior of darkside hackers has been called electronic terrorism.

8

Viruses, Worms, and Other Sinister Programs

By September 1998 there were some twenty thousand known computer viruses.[1] The number was growing by about one thousand new viruses per month.[2]

A virus is code or a piece of software designed to alter the way a computer works without the user's knowledge or consent. Viruses may be benign or malicious. Benign viruses usually cause no damage. For example, some past viruses were simply intended to be funny. One was called the "Cookie Monster." It flashed the message "I want a cookie" on the screen, and users had to "feed" the word cookie to the monster to keep it under control.

Malicious viruses cause unintentional or deliberate damage. (Unintentional damage is caused by programming errors.) They may alter a program so that it does not work as it should, or they may completely erase the hard disk.

Viruses reproduce themselves. They can make themselves known immediately, or a trigger, such as a date, time, or command word, can activate them. (These delayed reaction codes are called *logic bombs*.) In some cases, the virus runs undetected, simply making the machine sluggish or causing unexpected results when programs are run.

Types of Viruses

Viruses are classified according to the manner in which they infect computers:

Boot sector viruses are the most common. They attach themselves to the section of a floppy or hard disk that lets the user "boot up" to begin working with the computer. Boot sector viruses are most often spread by booting up the computer with an infected floppy disk in place. These viruses gain control as the computer is first turned on by moving from the boot sector of the floppy disk into the computer's memory. The virus can then infect the hard disk. At this point, any new disk placed in the floppy disk drive can also become infected.

File infectors replace or attach themselves to files with certain extensions (usually command or executable files with the extensions .COM and .EXE). Programs become infected when they are executed with the virus in memory. These viruses, if well written, operate without revealing their presence. Some reproduce until a certain date, such as Friday the 13th, then begin destroying files. Sometimes the only way to rid infected files of the virus is to delete them and reinstall the uninfected software.

Multipartite viruses are a combination of boot sector and file types. Because they infect both boot sectors and files, they are more easily spread. Variations of this type of virus, such as polymorphic and stealth viruses, are the most difficult to detect and delete. Polymorphic viruses keep changing in order to fool virus-scanner programs. Stealth viruses temporarily remove themselves from memory so that virus-scanners cannot find them.

Macro viruses, first discovered in 1995, infect documents created with Microsoft Word (version 6.0 and above) and Microsoft Excel, a spreadsheet application. Macro viruses infect spreadsheets, documents, and templates, which can be opened by either Windows or Macintosh applications.

A Microsoft Word macro virus, dubbed the Melissa virus, was apparently first introduced by being uploaded to the Internet Newsgroup alt.sex from a stolen America Online account on March 26, 1999. It spread through Microsoft's Outlook Express (an e-mail program) via an e-mail attachment. Once the attachment was opened, the virus grabbed names from the computer user's address book and sent itself to each name on the list. Because the fast-spreading virus could quickly clog, then crash, even the large mail servers, companies who were warned quickly shut down all outgoing mail. Within a few days, patches that could disable the virus were made available by antivirus software companies.[3]

In a matter of days, David L. Smith, a New Jersey man, was arrested and charged with writing and sending out the virus, which had already infected more than one hundred thousand computers worldwide. Still, in just a couple of days, the virus clogged and in some cases incapacitated computer networks at about three hundred corporations.[4]

Paths to Infection

Any computer that is turned on can catch a virus, usually by:

- *Sharing infected diskettes*. Boot sector viruses often spread from infected floppy disks left in the drive while rebooting.

- *CD-ROMS*. Presently, the CDs themselves cannot become infected, but the files they contain may be infected.

- *Downloading infected files*. These files are downloaded from bulletin boards or the Web.

- *Opening an infected e-mail attachment*. (Macro viruses make this possible.) The infection is in the attachment, not in the e-mail message.

- *Linked computers that are not protected by antivirus software*. Viruses can spread from infected files located on file servers and attached to e-mail.

Some Infamous Viruses

From 1989 to 1993, 160 viruses credited to Bulgaria were in circulation. During that time, 10 percent of all viruses in the United States came from that country. Viruses were posted and exchanged on a Bulgarian bulletin board, the Virus Exchange BBS. Many were created by someone called "Dark Avenger," who named a malicious virus after himself in 1989.

The virus Dark Avenger was epidemic in the United States. It attached itself to MS-DOS- .COM and .EXE files, adding 1,800 bytes of code. Every sixteenth time the infected program ran, it overwrote a section of the hard disk. Then a message appeared: "Eddie Lives . . . somewhere in time." Another message was embedded in the code: "This program was written in the city of Sofia ©1988–89 Dark Avenger." Infected computers eventually crashed after having lost part of their operating system.

For some unknown reason, after 1993 the Bulgarian virus factory ceased production. That year the Dark Avenger created his last malicious virus— Commander_Bomber.[5] Some thought he and his colleagues had found more legitimate uses for their skills.

After the first macro virus, called Concept, was introduced in June 1995, it soon became the most common virus in the world. When an infected Microsoft Word document was opened, the virus copied itself into the global document template (the file NORMAL.DOT). Thereafter, whenever a document was saved with Save-File-As, the virus copied itself into the saved document. The first time an infected document was opened, a box appeared with the title "Microsoft Word" and the number "1." The number was apparently supposed to increase each time the virus duplicated itself, but due to bugs in the program it never counted above 1.[6] From 1998 on, versions of Microsoft Word and Excel contained built-in antivirus code to prevent macro virus infections.

Other Sinister Programs

Some infectious computer programs are less deadly than viruses. For example, a worm, Robert Tappan Morris's toxin of choice, does not usually destroy data. It can reproduce itself and load up a computer's memory, however, causing it to crash.

Several other nuisance programs differ from viruses in that they do not reproduce themselves. The Trojan horse, for instance, is named for the fabled giant wooden horse in which Greek warriors were smuggled into Troy. True to its name, this program is disguised as innocent code, but it has a hidden purpose.

Members of the Inner Circle hackers' group used a Trojan horse concealed in a chess game to gain entry to a Canadian mainframe computer they had been trying to crack. They talked the system operator into playing the game with them. Then, while the chess program was running, it opened a powerful, unauthorized account in the host computer for the hackers to use later, undetected.[7]

The logic bomb, or time bomb, is similar to a

Trojan horse, but it is programmed to go off at a particular time. Logic bombs are the favorite device of angry employees intent on getting even. They can plant such a program and set it to go off and do damage sometime after they leave the company.

Trapdoors Can Let Intruders In

Trapdoors (also called "backdoors") allow others to penetrate a system, but they are not always created to cause damage. They are sometimes legitimate lines of code that are written into programs by programmers to provide an easy way in for maintenance. If the trapdoor is not closed after its purpose has been served, however, crackers can use it to gain unauthorized access.

Virus Control

Antiviral software scans programs or disks for viruses. Most antiviral programs can also erase viruses. The better programs scan for thousands of known viruses, and technical support is available for users.

When a virus can be traced to its originator, that person faces prosecution for illegal computer activity. A case in point is Christopher Pile (a.k.a. "Black Baron"), a virus writer in Great Britain who was not only arrested but also went to prison under that country's 1990 Computer Misuse Act. Pile, a twenty-seven-year-old unemployed, self-taught programmer, wrote two viruses called Pathogen and Queeg. A computer crime specialist spent ten months tracing the code back to Pile. At his trial in 1995, a

British company testified that it lost $1 million to damage caused by the viruses. Pile was convicted and sentenced to eighteen months in prison. The sentencing judge told Pile that "those who seek to wreak mindless havoc on one of the vital tools of our age cannot expect lenient treatment."[8]

An Apple a Day . . .

Here are a few tips to guard against virus infection:

- Use reliable sources for programs. Shareware posted for the taking on bulletin boards can be infected, so computer users who trade programs should be careful. Pirated copies of software can also contain a virus. Purchased programs in shrink-wrap are most likely to be virusfree, but there have been exceptions.

- Write-protect all the disks used, so no one can transmit a virus to them.

- If the system in use has a hard or fixed disk, never boot from a diskette.

- Make backup copies frequently.

- Watch for changes in the way a system works. Do programs take longer than usual to load? Do disk access times seem excessively long for the task to be performed? Are there unusual error messages? Is less system memory available than usual? Have programs or files mysteriously disappeared? Has available disk space been suddenly reduced? The presence of any one of these "symptoms" can indicate the presence of a virus.

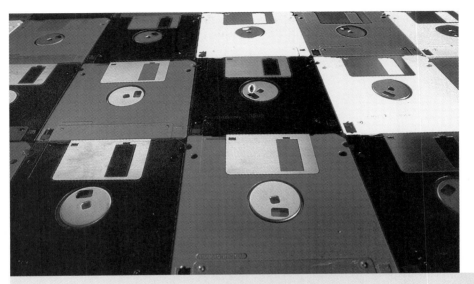

Making back-up copies of a computer's hard drive is one way to keep from losing months of valuable work.

- Do not run programs received in e-mail or open e-mail attachments unless you know exactly what they are and where they came from.

- Use a reliable antivirus program regularly to scan for viruses. Update the program at least once every eighteen months.

- When a virus is detected, tell others who might have used the same disks, to prevent further spread of the infection.

Virus Hoaxes

Virus hoaxes often circulate on the Internet. E-mail messages may tell recipients, "Just wanted to warn you about a new virus . . . Make sure you warn all your friends!" Most of these messages are untrue. At least one such message in 1998, however, was genuine. It warned some Internet users about a new computer virus called "RedTeam," which could spread via e-mail. The virus infected Windows executable files and the Windows kernel file. If it infected a computer running the Eudora e-mail program, it could use Eudora to send out an electronic mail message with an attached program. RedTeam was unusual because it could send e-mail with itself attached, and it could also circulate rumors about itself. The virus was not widely circulated, however, and it was easily contained simply by not opening the e-mail attachment that contained the code and by not forwarding the warning message to friends.[9]

E-mail messages circulated to warn others of "viruses" can take up Internet capacity and waste others' time. A better way to find out which viruses are a threat and which are hoaxes is to consult one of the several Web sites for that purpose.

Who Are the Virus Creators?

Since virus writers work in secret, profiling them is difficult. Researchers have found they are almost always male, many are high school or college students who have just taken their first programming course, and most are probably attracted by the fellowship of virus writing.[10]

Sarah Gordon, a researcher with IBM's Antivirus Laboratory, found that most virus writers grew out of the behavior by ages seventeen, eighteen, or nineteen. By the late 1990s, this was changing. Virus writers did not "age out" of the behavior as early as they had previously, and they had become "more malicious and intent." Motives for writing viruses, however, were as varied as the writers themselves.

Some common motives included curiosity, revenge, making a personal statement, and gaining the attention of peers.[11]

Whatever the motive for creating a virus or other destructive program, experts have compared the act to such crimes as "putting typhoid in the public water supply" or "picking up a baseball bat to break windows, instead of hitting balls." Victims of virus attacks agree that the destruction caused hardly justifies the few moments of satisfaction a virus's creator feels when his or her program works.

9

Laws and Civil Liberties in Cyberspace

In 1990, law enforcement officers hit hard at suspected crackers. In fourteen American cities in May 1990, Secret Service and police officers staged surprise raids, dubbed "Operation Sundevil." Armed with guns and search warrants, officers seized forty-two computers and 23,000 disks. They also shut down twenty-five electronic bulletin boards. The target of the roundup was a group of youthful crackers, many of them members of the Legion of Doom. They were suspected of trafficking in stolen credit-card numbers, telephone access codes, and other illegally obtained electronic information. At least one suspect, twenty-one-year-old

100

Robert Chandler, later pleaded guilty in federal court in California to a felony, possessing fifteen or more telephone access codes.[1] The raids did not result in scores of successful prosecutions, but they did put crackers on notice that law enforcement was serious about computer crime.

While not part of Operation Sundevil, a second raid in 1990 also made history. Two months before, on March 1, 1990, the Austin, Texas, offices of Steve Jackson Games were raided by the U.S. Secret Service. Apparently one of Jackson's employees was under investigation for hacker activities supposedly related to the *Phrack*/E911 incident. Agents had no evidence connecting the employee to his employer, however.

Although Jackson's games were marketed as books and were not sold on computer disks, the agents took computers, laser printers, and photocopy machines, as well as disks containing work in progress. When computers were seized, a bulletin board operated by the business was also shut down. No one was arrested or charged with any crime as a result of the raid on Steve Jackson Games. The business was seriously disrupted, however, and eventually half the staff was laid off.[2]

With the financial and legal help of the Electronic Frontier Foundation, a cyberliberties group formed in 1990, Jackson sued the United States Secret Service. In March 1993 a federal judge ruled in favor of Steve Jackson Games. He said that under the Privacy Protection Act of 1980, the publisher's work product had been illegally seized and held. (The Privacy Protection Act says that it is illegal for the government, while conducting a criminal investigation, to search for or seize "work product" related to books, newspapers, or other "public communication" without probable cause.)

The judge also ruled that Secret Service agents had violated the Electronic Communications Privacy Act by unlawfully reading, disclosing, and erasing computer messages on a bulletin board run by Steve Jackson Games. A year after the judgment, Jackson received $52,431 for lost profits and direct costs of the raid. The government also agreed to pay costs of the suit, at $252,405.[3]

After the 1990 raids, several constitutional questions were raised. Were the electronic bulletin boards shut down in the raids entitled to protection under the First Amendment in the same way as the words on a printed page? When computers and disks were seized, were citizens deprived of "life, liberty, or property, without due process of law," as prohibited by the Fifth Amendment?

Electronic privacy and security also emerged as critical issues. How can citizens protect their privacy when every telephone call, credit card charge, and cash-card transaction is recorded electronically? Who owns such information? What happens to property rights when documents can be digitally reproduced to look exactly like the original?

Encryption

One way to ensure privacy is to encrypt online data. Encryption uses a special chip or software that codes or scrambles computer transmissions so that others cannot read them. The coded data can only be unscrambled by a decode key. Encryption uses either secret keys or public keys. Secret key encryption uses a single decoding key shared by two communicating parties. Public key encryption uses a public key and a private key. The public key is known by everyone, but it cannot be modified. The private key is kept secret. Data encoded with the public key can be decoded only when the private key is supplied.

In 1977 the National Security Agency worked with IBM to create a secret key Data Encryption Standard (DES), which was adopted by the United States Department of Defense for use in coding online data. By 1998 DES had become the most widely used method of encrypting data to protect financial trans- actions, medical records, and other sensitive information. The key was judged so difficult to break that it was restricted by the United States government for exportation to other countries. The code was diffi- cult to break without the private key, because there were 72 quadrillion or more possible keys that could be used. For each given message, the key was chosen at random. Both the sender and the receiver would have to know and use the same private key.

In a record-breaking feat in July 1998, John Gilmore, a civil liberties activist, and Paul Kocher, a cryptographer, cracked DES. They built a $250,000 computer (financed by the Electronic Frontier Foundation) that searched through 88 billion keys per second and in just fifty-six hours found the one that worked.[4]

In 1993 scientists at the U. S. National Security Agency invented a chip that they claimed could generate uncrackable codes. With computer crime on the rise, the government touted the "Clipper chip" as the answer to secure telecommunications. The catch, however, was that the government would have the key to decode data. This would let law enforcement officials monitor computer and telephone transmissions without the senders' knowledge. The Clipper chip had many critics, and when it was discovered that decoding keys did not always work, it was not adopted for widespread use.[5]

The debate continued over the security of the DES encryption system and the Clipper chip. In the meantime, others were developing alternate methods of making telecommunications more private. Here are two that were in common use in 1998:

- *Pretty Good Privacy (PGP)*: A public key encryption code written by Paul Zimmerman in 1991. PGP was free, and by 1998 it was used by private citizens worldwide.

- *Digital Signature Standard (DSS)*: Since documents created online cannot be signed by hand, codes were developed for digital signatures. To identify and authenticate the signer, two codes were used. One code was used when the person "signed" the document; another was used to decode the "signature." DSS assured a receiver that the message was not a forgery, but it did not provide confidentiality of information.

The State of Computer Security

It is true that computer systems with excellent security are the least likely to be cracked. Yet, despite recent security product developments, some computer networks are becoming more, not less, vulnerable to outside attack:

"I know about 95 percent of [the vulnerabilities] I am going to find at a company before I even get there. I can steal a billion dollars from any [corporation] within a couple of hours," said Ira Winkler, president of the Information Security Advisory Group, a company that contracts to attack business systems to find security holes.[6]

"The average system out there uses out-of-the-box software . . . which has extremely poor quality, lack of patches, no security. And these systems are not well maintained or configured. Plus, there is now a wide array of automated hacking tools available. It is pretty much a no-brainer to get into these systems," said Eugene Spafford, director of the Cerias Center for Education in Research, Information Assurance and Security at Purdue University, West Lafayette, Indiana.[7]

"We try to see what we can do when we break into a system. Can we see secret data, can we fake e-mail from the CEO to all employees giving them a day off? Is anyone even aware we are breaking in? In many of the companies we break into, nobody even raises a red flag. In fact, we break in about 80 percent of the time," said Charles C. Palmer, manager of network security and cryptography at IBM's Watson Research

Center. Palmer's group is paid by companies to find security lapses by breaking into their systems.[8]

Passwords, Biometrics, and Other High-Tech Locks

Passwords can be the first step toward locking out unauthorized computer users. Often they are the weakest link in the security chain, however, because they are too easy to guess. Obvious bad choices are the user's name, birth dates, nicknames, and other easily guessed personal facts.

The most secure passwords, security experts advise, are chosen from a set of random characters such as *(?SOV#! Passwords should never be posted in obvious places, such as near computer workstations or on bulletin boards, and they should be changed often.

Biometrics does not rely on passwords. Instead, it uses physical traits, such as fingerprints, voice prints, or blood vessel patterns in the eye, to identify the computer operator.

Other security measures include software created to detect security holes in a system, and firewalls. Firewalls are powerful Internet gateway computers that protect a network by filtering incoming and outgoing transactions.

Vigilant humans are vital to security. System administrators and users should pay close attention to the machine's behavior. Is an account being heavily used? Are there logged messages that someone is exceeding authorization? Is someone logging on who does not have proper authorization? Is someone assigned to read logs and note inconsistencies?

Cyberethics

As computer use (and misuse) has increased, ethics, or responsible use of systems, has become more important. Many organizations for computer professionals now have written codes of ethics that members are expected to follow. For example, the Association for Computing Machinery (ACM), the Institute of Electrical and Electronics Engineers (IEEE), the National Society of Professional Engineers (NSPE), the Data Processing Management Association (DPMA), and the International Federation for Information Processing (IFIP) all have professional codes of ethics. Societies in other countries that have written codes of ethics include the Hong Kong Computer Society, the Assistive Devices Industry Association of Canada, and the Australian Computer Society.

Many universities have also begun to deal with the ethics issue. For example, the University of Virginia has posted online an ethics statement for students. It poses these questions: What is sexual harassment over the Internet? Should misidentification, plagiarism, and misinformation be somehow limited or involve punishment? Can these problems be handled without infringing on the privacy of others? Is hacking always wrong? If a student breaks into a system, is he or she obligated to tell the company or institution that they are "crackable"? Should everyone be allotted the same amount of usage/bandwidth,

Charles C. Palmer, manager of network security and cryptography at IBM's Watson Research Center, heads a group that contracts with companies to find security lapses by breaking into their systems. By fixing the lapses, companies can stop intruders from breaking into their computers.

or should it depend on need? Should everyone have the same access to research information? If not, what will determine "information haves" and "have-nots"? When is use of university computers inappropriate? For instance, could a student write a book using school facilities and keep all royalties? And should students play games with their computers, tying up "public" bandwidth in the process?[9]

Most experts claim that the answers to cyberethics questions lie in legal penalties for criminal abuses and in early education of computer users. According to Eugene Spafford, early access to computers does not help teach responsible use, unless young users have guidance. "Access to computers without tradition, without guidance, without understanding can lead some people into trouble."[10]

In 1998, IBM's Sarah Gordon noticed a disturbing trend while visiting a theme park.

> One attraction was geared for youngsters to experience computing. A video showed two students breaking away from their classmates on a school trip. They said, 'Let's just sneak off and see what we can do.' They broke into a locked computer room using a key card, broke into a network, and went through e-mail and personal documents. Then they came back to their group and told their classmates. When the teacher asked them how they had learned all that information, a little girl winked at the camera and said, 'It's all out there; it's part of the network.' I thought what a terrible message to send to thousands of kids a day. . . . These mixed messages sent to kids as they are learning to interact with computer technologies can be harmful. Students can forget

that there are people on the other end of those modems and computers.[11]

Guidelines for Ethical Computing

By following a few simple guidelines, computer users can ensure their own rights to privacy, as well as those of others. The Computer Ethics Institute says never use a computer to:

- harm other people;
- interfere with the computer work of others;
- snoop around in the computer files of others;
- steal;
- issue false statements;
- copy or use proprietary software without paying for it;
- use the computer resources of others without their authorization or without proper compensation;
- steal the intellectual products of others.

When using a computer:

- think about the social consequences of the programs you write or the systems you design; and
- find ways to use the machine that ensure consideration and respect for others.[12]

Like locks on houses, security measures can keep out unwanted computer intruders. But, as is true for all crime prevention, the best barrier to computer crime will always be educated, responsible users.

Glossary

binary code—The programs that run computers are made up of a complex series of 1s and Os, called a binary code.

binary digit—Either a 1 or a O—represented by low-voltage and high-voltage current applied to switches (transistors) inside the microchips of a computer. Also called a bit (binary digit).

boot infector—A type of computer virus that attaches itself to that section of a floppy or hard disk that allows the computer to boot up, or load operating programs.

bootlegging—Making copies of commercial software for illegal resale.

bulletin board—A means of exchanging information online via modem by posting it to a host computer.

byte—A byte equals eight bits or binary digits and is the basic unit of measuring memory in computing.

carders—Hackers who steal credit card numbers for resale or for personal use.

central processing unit (CPU)—The computer's brain. Part of the system unit, the CPU runs the programs that tell a computer which functions to perform.

computer languages—Short letter combinations used by programmers to relay instructions to computers.

computer security—Methods used to keep unauthorized users out of a computer system.

cracker—Slang term for someone who gains unauthorized entry into a computer system.

cyberethics—A term for the ethics (matters concerned with right and wrong) of computer use.

cyberspace—A term for computer networks coined by science-fiction writer William Gibson.

data diddling—Changing data going into a computer or coming out of a computer without authorization.

disk drive—Reads and writes information to or from a diskette.

diskette—A floppy or removable computer disk.

Dumpster diving—Sifting through trash to get unauthorized information about a computer system.

encryption—A method of scrambling computer communication to keep it private.

fixed disk—Also called a hard disk. The fixed disk cannot be removed from the computer; holds more information than a removable, or floppy, diskette.

gigabyte—A unit of measurement for computer memory that equals one billion bytes.

hacker—An expert at operating a computer.

hardware—The physical equipment that makes up a computer system.

Internet—A complex system of computer networks developed in the mid–1980s.

kilobyte (K)—A unit of measurement for computer memory that equals 1,024 bytes.

logic bomb—Code that tells the computer to perform a certain function at a certain time.

megabyte (Mb)—A unit of measurement for computer memory that equals 1,048,576 bytes.

megahertz—A unit for measuring the speed of a computer that equals one million hertz.

microchip—See **microprocessor**.

microprocessor—Also called **microchip**. Tiny wafers of silicon containing a series of electrical circuits. They relay the electrical impulses that operate the computer.

multipartite viruses—A combination of boot sector and file types. They infect both boot sectors and files, which means they are more easily spread.

network—A system that allows linked computers to exchange information.

online—The term used for communication with another computer.

password—A code word or phrase that allows users to gain access to shared computer files.

personal identification number (PIN)—A number assigned to credit card, telephone calling card, and automatic teller machine users that lets them access their account.

phone phreaks—A slang term for computer users who gain unauthorized entry into computer systems used by the telephone company.

piggybacking—Obtaining another's personal identification number by looking over his or her shoulder while a transaction is in progress. See also **shoulder-surfing**.

private branch–exchange (PBX)—A phone system used by businesses that allows employees to dial into the home office on an "800" (toll-free) line, then use a PIN to dial long-distance.

salami slicing—Occurs when a computer operator steals small amounts from a large number of sources, through electronic changing of data (like slicing thin pieces from a roll of salami).

shareware—Programs shared by computer operators through electronic exchange.

shoulder-surfing—Stealing personal identification numbers by looking over the shoulders of legitimate customers while they access their accounts. See also **piggybacking**.

social engineering—Using charm to acquire privileged information.

software—Instructions that make a computer perform its various functions.

software piracy—Stealing software, either for resale or for personal use.

system infector—A type of computer virus that gains control after the computer is booted up. It affects some operating system files.

time bomb—See **logic bomb**.

trapdoors—Holes written into software programs that give programmers and/or intruders a way in.

trashing—See **Dumpster diving**.

Trojan horse—A destructive computer program disguised as an innocent one.

virus—Destructive code that reproduces itself inside a computer and destroys or alters data.

wire fraud—A criminal act that uses the telephone system to steal or extort money or information.

World Wide Web—A system that links Internet documents, making them easier to locate. Also called the Web, WWW, and W3.

worm—Computer code that reproduces itself like a virus, but usually does not destroy data.

Y2K—Slang for the year 2000.

Chapter Notes

Chapter 1. Arrested!

1. Dan Meriwether, "Kevin Mitnick: An Excerpt From Takedown," 1995, <http://www.takedown.com/bio/mitnick.html> (December 9, 1998).

2. Katie Hafner and John Markoff, *Cyberpunk—Outlaws and Hackers on the Computer Frontier* (New York: Simon & Schuster, 1991), pp. 102, 344.

3. John Schwartz, "Inside the Head of a Hacker," *Newsweek*, July 29, 1991.

4. John Markoff, "How a Computer Sleuth Traced a Digital Trail," *The New York Times*, February 15, 1995, <http://www.takedown.com/coverage/digital-trail.html> (December 8, 1998).

5. Dan Meriwether, "Timeline," 1995, <http://www.takedown.com/timeline/index/html> (December 9, 1998).

6. Jean Guisnel, *Cyberwars: Espionage on the Internet* (New York: Plenum Trade, 1997), p. 131.

7. Dan Meriwether, "Voicemail," 1995, <http://www.takedown.com/timeline/capture/index.html> (March 10, 1999).

8. Christopher Sullivan, "Taking a Byte Out of Crime," *Minneapolis Star Tribune*, February 18, 1995, p. 1D.

9. Elizabeth Weise, "Feared Hacker Fined $4,125, Could Be Freed in January," *USA Today*, August 11, 1999, p. D1.

Chapter 2. Computerizing Society

1. Mark K. Anderson, "Y2K," *Valley Advocate*, New Mass Media, Inc., <http://www.valleyadvocate.com/articles/y2k.html> (July 12, 1998).

2. Steve Nelson, "ENIAC," *Microsoft Encarta Encyclopedia 99*, 1993–1998 Microsoft Corporation.

3. Roberta L. Baher and Marilyn Wertheimer Meyer, *Computer in Your Future 98* (Indianapolis, IN: Que Education and Training, 1998), p. 33.

4. Gary Master, "Computers," *Microsoft, Encarta 96 Encyclopedia*, 1993–1995, Microsoft Corporation, p. 7 of printout.

5. *The Computerized Society* (Alexandria, Va.: Time–Life Books, 1987), pp. 23–24.

6. John McAfee and Colin Haynes, *Computer Viruses, Worms, Data Diddlers, Killer Programs, and Other Threats to Your System* (New York: St. Martin's Press, 1989), p. 29.

7. David H. Freedman and Charles C. Mann, *@Large: The Strange Case of the World's Biggest Internet Invasion* (New York: Simon & Schuster, 1997), pp. 69–70.

8. David Shenk, *Data Smog: Surviving the Information Glut* (New York: HarperCollins, 1997), p. 84.

9. "Current Internet Statistics," <http://www.ipdnet.com/statistics.htm> (December 14, 1998).

10. Electronic Frontier Foundation, "The Open Platform" [a report] (Cambridge, Mass.: Electronic Frontier Foundation: 1992), p. 4.

11. Jennifer Tanaka, "Zippy Trips on the Web, *Newsweek*, July 6, 1998, p. 48.

12. Chris Allbritton, "Superhighway Getting Fast Lane," *Rapid City Journal*, January 21, 1998, p. A3.

13. August Bequai, *Techno-Crimes: The Computerization of Crime and Terrorism* (Lexington, Mass.: Lexington Books, 1987), p. 52.

14. Donn B. Parker, *Crime by Computer* (New York: Charles Scribner's Sons, 1976), pp. 14, 18.

15. McAfee and Haynes, p. 7.

16. Michelle Slatalla and Joshua Quittner, *Masters of Deception: The Gang That Ruled Cyberspace* (New York: HarperCollins, 1995), pp. 1–4.

17. Hal Abelson, Mike Fischer, and Joanne Costello, "6.805/STS085: Readings on Computer Crime," November 9, 1997, <http://swissnet.ai.mit.edu/6095/readings-crime.html> (July 15, 1998).

18. Robert Uhlig, "Hackers Sabotage Blair's Internet Image," *The Telegraph*, December 10, 1996, <http://www.sotmesc.org/phrack/P50-15> (August 19, 1998).

19. Richard M. Stallman, "Letter to ACM Forum," *Communications of the ACM*, vol. 27, no. 1, January 1984, pp. 8–9.

20. Abelson, Fischer, and Costello, "6.805/STSO85: Readings on Computer Crime."

21. T. Trent Gegax, "Stick 'Em Up? Not Anymore. Now It's Crime by Keyboard," *Newsweek*, July 21, 1997, p. 14.

22. John Larrabee, "Cyberspace a New Beat for Police," *USA Today*, April 26, 1994, p. 2A.

23. Scott Charney and Kent Alexander, "Computer Crime," September 22, 1997, <http://www.law.emory.edu/ELJ/volumes/sum96/alex.html> (July 10, 1998).

24. Tim Wilson, "Profits Embolden Hackers," *TechWeb*, March 23, 1998, <http://www.techweb.com/wire/story/TWB19980323S0013> (March 10, 1999).

25. Ibid.

Chapter 3. Hacking U.S.A.

1. Douglas Thomas (professor at the Annenberg School for Communication, columnist for *Online Journalism Review, author of Hacking Culture*, and a former hacker), interview with the author, August 3, 1998.

2. Willis Marti (senior lecturer and director of computing and facilities services group, Texas A & M University, College Station, Texas), interview with author, September 9, 1998.

3. Eugene Spafford (professor of computer sciences, Purdue University), interview with author, August 19, 1998.

4. Ibid.

5. Douglas Thomas interview.

6. Douglas Thomas, "Hackers as Watchdogs of Industry," *Online Journalism Review*, February 17, 1998, <http://olj.usc.edu/sections/departments/98_stories> (July 17, 1998).

7. Douglas Thomas, "Sorting Out the Hacks and the Hackers," *Online Journalism Review*, March 31, 1998,

<http://olj.usc.edu/sections/departments/98_stories> (July 17, 1998).

8. Bruce Sterling, *The Hacker Crackdown—Law and Disorder on the Electronic Frontier* (New York: Bantam Books, 1992), p. 77.

9. Bruce Sterling (science-fiction author and author of *The Hacker Crackdown*), interview with author, August 21, 1998.

10. Ibid.

11. Press Release, PricewaterhouseCoopers, "Global Information Security Survey Reflects IT Professionals' Views Worldwide," August 31, 1998.

12. "Large corporations now see outside security threat," audio of interview conducted by Laura DiDio, senior editor at *Computer World*, with Mark Gembicki, president of WarRoom Research LLC, a security consultancy based in Annapolis, MD, August 17, 1998, <http://www.computerworld.com/home/features.nsf/all/980817gambecki> (March 10, 1999).

13. Harold Hendershot (supervisory special agent, Computer Fraud and Abuse, FBI), interview with author, January 19, 1993.

14. Scott Charney (chief of the Computer Crime Unit, U.S. Department of Justice), interview with author, January 6, 1993.

15. Dora Winter (information technology dept., University of Michigan, Ann Arbor), interview with author, August 24, 1998.

16. Hal Abelson, Mike Fischer, and Joanne Costello,"6.805/STS085: Readings on Computer Crime," November 9, 1997, <http://swissnet.ai.mit.edu/6095/readings-crime.html> (July 15, 1998).

Chapter 4. Stealing Money

1. Christine Dugas, "FBI Cybercops Hunt Hackers: Agents Armed With Laptops Nab Robbers," *USA Today*, March 3, 1998, pp. 1B–2B.

2. Ibid., p. 2B.

3. *Chicago Tribune*, "MCI Worker in Phone-card Ripoff," October 4, 1994, <http://eff.bilkent.edu.tr/

pub/Legal/Cases/lay_mci_phonecard_theft_case.note>
(March 10, 1999).

4. *New York Times News Service* and Nando.net,
"Social Security Info Used by Stolen Credit-Card Ring,"
April 6, 1996, <http://www.nando.net/newsroom/
ntn/info/040696/info5_14984.html> (July 10, 1998).

5. Hal Abelson, Mike Fischer, and Joanne Costello,
"6.805/STSO85: Readings on Computer Crime,"
November 15, 1997, <http://swissnet.ai.mit.edu/
6095/readings-crime.html> (July 10, 1998).

6. Barbara E. McMullen and John F. McMullen,
"Companies Fall Victim to Massive PBX Fraud,"
Newsbytes, April 20, 1992, <http://www.fc.net/
phrack/files/p39/p39-10.html> (August 18, 1998).

7. T. Trent Gegax, "Stick 'Em Up? Not Anymore. Now
It's Crime by Keyboard," *Newsweek*, July 21, 1997,
p. 14.

8. "Computer Crime," case summaries, May 1, 1995,
<http://www.eff.org/pub/Legal/comp_crime_cases.
summaries> (August 15, 1998).

9. Alexandra Alger, "Carte Blanche for Crooks," *Forbes*,
December 2, 1996, <http://www.forbes.com/forbes/
120296/5813272a.htm> (July 21, 1998).

10. Ibid.

11. Ibid.

12. Ibid.

13. Barbara E. McMullen and John F. McMullen.

14. Neil Orman, "Fighting Check Fraud," *Austin
Business Journal*, September 16, 1996, <http://www.
amcity.com/austin/stories/091696/focus1.html>
(August 25, 1998).

15. W. Power and C. Torres, "Stocks Drop as Salomon
Clerk Errs," *Wall Street Journal*, March 26, 1992, p. C1.

16. T. Trent Gegax, p. 14.

17. Lynn Van Dine, "Crooks Lurk Behind Phony Web
Sites," *The Detroit News*, February 25, 1997,
<http://detnews.com/cyberia/sites/970225/crooks/
crooks.htm> (July 15, 1998).

18. Alan Sangster Web page (School of Management of the Queen's University of Belfast Web site),"Controlling Computer Crime, Incompetence and Carelessness," *Salami-style Embezzlement*, <http://www.qub.ac.uk/mgt/alans/ais97/ba420/crime/crime.htm> (July 15, 1998).

19. Rogue Agent, "City of London Surrenders to Cyber Gangs," The London *Times*, June 2, 1996, <http://www.datasync.com/~sotmesc/news/cybterr.txt> (July 15, 1998).

Chapter 5. Information Profiteers

1. Donn B. Parker, *Fighting Computer Crime* (New York: Charles Scribner's Sons, 1983), pp. 177–178.

2. Bruce Sterling, *The Hacker Crackdown—Law and Disorder on the Electronic Frontier* (New York: Bantam Books, 1992), p. vii.

3. Steve Ditlea, *Digital Deli* (New York: Workman Publishing, 1984), pp. 59–60.

4. Katie Hafner and John Markoff, *Cyberpunk— Outlaws and Hackers on the Computer Frontier* (New York: Simon & Schuster, 1991), p. 19.

5. Andrew Craig, "Telecom Fraud Software Looks and Learns," *Internet Week*, April 29, 1998, <http://www.techweb.com/wire/story/TWB19980429S00010> (July 21, 1998).

6. Larry Kahaner, "Carriers Arm Themselves to Fight Fraud," *TechWeb*, February 2, 1998, <http://www.techweb.com/wire/se/directlink.cgi?INW19980202S0019> (March 10, 1999).

7. Paul Keegan, "High-Tech Pirates Collecting Phone Calls," *USA Today*, September 23, 1994, p. 4A.

8. Christine Dugas, "Visa: Card Fraud at All-Time Low," *USA Today*, February 16, 1998, p. 1B.

9. Jonathan Littman, "The FBI Takes on Hackers," *CNET, Inc.*, November 20, 1997, <http://www.singapore.cnet.com/Briefs/Guidebook/Finest/index.html> (July 15, 1998).

10. Carol Levin, "Trading Cards," *PC Magazine* online, February 27, 1998, <http://search.zdnet.com/pcmag/news/trends/t980227a.htm> (July 28, 1998).

11. Ibid.

12. "Controlling Computer Crime, Incompetence and Carelessness," <http://www.qub.ac.uk/mgt/alans/ais97/ba420/crime.crime.htm> (July 15, 1998).

13. Shari Steele, staff attorney, "Classifying Hobbyist Electronic Bulletin Boards" (Cambridge, Mass.: Electronic Frontier Foundation, 1992), p. 1.

14. News Release, U.S. Attorney for the District of New Jersey, "Cybersnare Sting," Department of Justice, September 11, 1995, <http://www.usdoj.gov/usao/nj/news/1995press/nj62.txt.html> (July 28, 1998).

Chapter 6. Pranksters and Pirates

1. "Aolhacks," posted August 22, 1998, <http://www.aolwatch.org/fanhack2.htm> (August 25, 1998).

2. Jonathan Littman, *The Watchman: The Twisted Life and Crimes of Serial Hacker Kevin Poulsen* (New York: Little, Brown and Company, 1997), pp. 14–15.

3. Gregory L. Vistica and Evan Thomas, "The Secret Hacker Wars," *Newsweek*, June 1, 1998, p. 60.

4. Andrew Quinn, "Teen Hackers Plead Guilty to Pentagon Attacks," *Time*, July 30, 1998, <http://cgi.pathfinder.com/time/daily/latest/RB/1998Jul30/39.html> (August 10, 1998).

5. Chris Taylor, "Justice a la Modem," *Time*, July 30, 1998, <http://cgi.pathfinder.com/ time/daily/0,2960,14233,00.html> (August 10, 1998).

6. Vistica and Thomas.

7. Darryl K. Taft, "No Electronic Theft," *Computer Reseller News*, September 29, 1977, <http://www.techweb.com/se/directlink.cgi?CRN19970929S0099> (March 10, 1999).

8. David McCandless, "Warez Wars," *Wired*, April 1997, <http://www.wired.com/wired/archive/5.04ff_warez.html?pg=2&topic=> (March 10, 1999).

9. Bruce Haring, "Cybermusic Pirates Agree to Stop Pilfering," *USA Today*, January 22, 1998, p. 1D.

Chapter 7. Darkside Hacking

1. Jonathan Littman, *The Watchman: The Twisted Life and Crimes of Serial Hacker Kevin Poulsen* (New York: Little, Brown and Company, 1997), p. 284.

2. "Prosecuting Computer Criminals Using State Computer Crime Statutes," Electronic Frontier Foundation case file, February 6, 1995, <http://www.eff.org/pub/Legal/prosecuting_computer_criminals.article> (July 15, 1998).

3. Philip Elmer-Dewitt, "Terror on the Internet," *Time*, December 12, 1994, <http://cgi.pathfinder.com/time/daily/archive/1994/941212/941212.technology.html> (August 3, 1998).

4. Joshua Quittner, "Invasion of Privacy," *Time*, August 25, 1997, <http://cgi.pathfinder.com/time/daily/magazine/1997/dom/970825/nation.invasion of p.html> (August 3, 1998).

5. Gary Strauss, "Employees, Ex-Workers Get Even," *USA Today*, August 20, 1998, p. 2B.

6. Ibid.

7. John Borland, "AlterNIC founder Headed for Extradition and U.S. Courts," Net Insider, December 18, 1997, <http://www.techweb.com/wire/story/TWB1997121850006> (August 12, 1998).

8. Bruce V. Bigelow, "To Some Hackers, Right and Wrong Don't Compute," *San Diego Union-Tribune*, May 11, 1992, <http://www.fc.net/phrack/files/p39/p39-10.html> (July 10, 1998).

9. Bill Landreth, *Out of the Inner Circle—A Hacker's Guide to Computer Security* (Bellevue, Wash.: Microsoft Press, 1985), pp. 35, 36.

10. Katie Hafner and John Markoff, *Cyberpunk: Outlaws and Hackers on the Computer Frontier* (New York: Simon & Schuster, 1991), p. 249.

11. Chris Taylor, "Hackers Plunder NASA, Pentagon," *Time*, April 23, 1998, <http://cgi.pathfinder.com/time/daily/article/0,2960,10997,00.html> (March 10, 1999).

12. Judy DeHaven, "High-Tech World Faces Low-Life Realities," *The Detroit News*, January 10, 1996, <http://detnews.com/cyberia/9601/daily/crime.html> (July 21, 1998).

Chapter 8. Viruses, Worms, and Other Sinister Programs

1. Sarah Gordon interview with author, September 8, 1998.

2. Matt Richtel, "Virus Hunters: Stalking 'Disease' on the Net," *The New York Times*, September 15, 1998, <http://www.nytimes.com> (September 20, 1998).

3. Stan Miastkowski, "How to Protect Yourself Against Melissa," CNN Online, March 29, 1999, <http://www.cnn.com/TECH/computing/9903/29/melissa.02.idg/index.html> (April 6, 1999).

4. David Kocieniewski, "Man Is Charged in the Creation of E-Mail Virus," April 3, 1999, pp. A1, B6.

5. David S. Bennahum, "Heart of Darkness," *Wired*, November 1997, posted June 1998, <http://www.wired.com/wired> (July 13, 1998).

6. IBM Antivirus Web site, <http://www.av.ibm.com/BreakingNews/VirusAlert/Concept> (September 20, 1998).

7. Bill Landreth, *Out of the Inner Circle—A Hacker's Guide to Computer Security* (Bellevue, Wash.: Microsoft Press, 1985), pp. 95–97.

8. "Profile of a Virus Writer, *PC World*, March 1997, <http://www.pcworld.com/software/utility/articles/mar97/1503p180w.html> (September 15, 1998).

9. IBM Antivirus Web site, <http://www.av.ibm.com/BreakingNews/VirusAlert/RedTeam> (September 20, 1998).

10. "Profile of a Virus Writer."

11. Sarah Gordon interview with author, September 8, 1998.

Chapter 9. Laws and Civil Liberties in Cyberspace

1. Michael Alexander, "Operation Sundevil Nabs First Suspect," *Computerworld*, February 17, 1992, p. 15.

2. Steve Jackson, "The Top Ten Media Errors About the SJ Games Raid," Electronic Frontier Foundation, February 12, 1992, <http://www.eff.org/pub.Legal/Intellectual_property/Legal/Cases/SJG/media_errors.sjg>(July 18, 1998).

3. Press Release: "Secret Service Pays Damages to Steve Jackson Games," Electronic Frontier Foundation, May 5, 1994, <http://www.eff.org/pub/Legal/Intellectual_property/Legal/Cases/SJG/SS_pays_sjg. announce> (March 10, 1999).

4. John Schwartz, "One High-End PC Cracks Data-Scrambling System," *Washington Post*, July 18, 1998, p. AO9.

5. Sharon Begley with Melinda Liu, "Foiling the Clipper Chip," *Newsweek*, June 13, 1994, pp. 60, 62.

6. Tim Wilson, "Profits Embolden Hackers," *TechWeb*, March 23, 1998, <http://www.techweb.com/wire/story/TWB19980323S0013> (March 10, 1999).

7. Eugene Spafford interview with author, May 7, 1991.

8. Charles C. Palmer interview with author, September 8, 1998.

9. "Ethics and the Internet," <http://minerva.acc. virginia.edu/~usem171/feb22/main.html> (September 15, 1998).

10. Eugene Spafford interview.

11. Sarah Gordon interview with author, September 8, 1998.

12. Computer Ethics Institute, "The Ten Commandments of Computer Ethics," December 4, 1997, <http://www.cpsr.org/program/ethics/cei.html> (March 10, 1999).

Further Reading

Banks, Michael A. *How to Protect Yourself in Cyberspace: Web Psychos, Stalkers, and Pranksters*. Albany, N.Y.: Coriolis Group Books, 1997.

De Angelis, Gina, and B. Marvis. *Cyber Crimes (Crime, Justice, and Punishment)*. New York: Chelsea House, 1999.

Forester, Tom, and Perry Morrison. *Computer Ethics: Cautionary Tales & Ethical Dilemmas in Computing*. Upland, Pa.: DIANE Publishing Co., 1998.

Gralla, Preston. *Complete Idiot's Guide to Protecting Yourself Online*. Indianapolis: Que Education and Training, 1999.

Kroen, William C. *Hackers No More*. New York: Random House, 1994.

Parker, Donn B. *Fighting Computer Crime: A New Framework for Protecting Information*. New York: John Wiley & Sons, 1998.

Stoll, Clifford. *Silicon Snake Oil: Second Thoughts on the Information Highway*. New York: Doubleday, 1995.

Internet Addresses

Computer Virus Myths Home Page
<http://www.kumite.com:80/myths/>

The Electronic Frontier Foundation
<http://www.eff.org>

Electronic Privacy Information Center
<http://epic.org/>

IBM Antivirus Web Site
<http://www.av.ibm.com>

Internet Newsletter
<http://www.ljextra.com/netnews>

Microsoft Security Advisor
<http://www.microsoft.com/security/>

PC Magazine
<http://www.zdnet.com/pcmag/>

Phrack
<http://www.2600.com/phrack>

Symantec AntiVirus Research Center
<http://www.symantec.com/avcenter/vinfodb.html>

2600, The Hacker Quarterly
<http://www.2600.com>

Wired
<http://www.wired.com/wired/>

Y2K News
<http://y2knews.com/>

Index